There was silence for such *there was a problem with Carl's antique cell phone. Finally, Rose asked, "And so what happens if you get pregnant, and you're too young to actually have a baby?"*

Defying all laws of inertia, the acceleration of Kennedy's heart rate crashed to a halt like a car plowing into a brick wall. "What do you mean?"

"Like, what if you're too young but you still get pregnant?"

"How young?" Kennedy spoke both words clearly and slowly, as if rushing might drive the timid voice away for good.

"Like thirteen."

Praise for *Unplanned*
by Alana Terry

"Deals with **one of the most difficult situations a pregnancy center could ever face**. The message is **powerful** and the story-telling **compelling**." ~ William Donovan, *Executive Director Anchorage Community Pregnancy Center*

"Alana Terry does an amazing job tackling a very **sensitive subject from the mother's perspective**." ~ Pamela McDonald, *Director Okanogan CareNet Pregnancy Center*

"**Thought-provoking** and intense ... Shows **different sides of the abortion argument**." ~ Sharee Stover, *Wordy Nerdy*

"Alana has a way of sharing the gospel **without being preachy**." ~ Phyllis Sather, *Purposeful Planning*

Note: The views of the characters in this novel do not necessarily reflect the views of the author.

The characters in this book are fictional. Any resemblance to real persons is coincidental. No part of this book may be reproduced in any form (electronic, audio, print, film, etc.) without the author's written consent.

www.alanaterry.com

Paralyzed

a novel by Alana Terry

"Whoever dwells in the shelter of the Most High
will rest in the shadow of the Almighty."

Psalm 91:1

CHAPTER 1

Loud.

Why was it so loud? Kennedy's knee-high boots clicked against the hard floor of the science hall. She glanced over one shoulder and then the other. Who was staring at her? She sensed his presence, felt his eyes — ominous black beams boring into her soul. She looked around, but all she could see was the crowds of students, milling, giggling, oblivious to fear and danger.

She should warn someone. There had to be almost a hundred students filing into the lecture hall to take their chemistry final. Didn't they know someone was watching them, waiting for them? No, waiting for her. Everyone else was safe. Kennedy was his only target. She glanced behind her.

Her imagination, or something far more insidious?

She longed for the days when stress meant finishing a paper by its deadline. There had been a time when her biggest frustration was working out a calculus equation so her TA wouldn't get mad at her for not showing her work. Was it really only six weeks ago that her little safety bubble had imploded around her?

When she left China to head for college last August, she had expected drama. Occasional tiffs with her roommate. Maybe a little dating awkwardness. The loneliness that would come from being on the other side of the world from her missionary parents. She was ready for that, just as she had been ready for the academics. She hadn't graduated first in her high school class by sitting around texting her friends or streaming videos all day. When she got off that plane last fall and took the airport shuttle to Harvard, when she tipped the driver and rolled her two suitcases up the stairs to her dorm, she had felt mature. Adventurous.

She was prepared.

Kennedy clutched her book to her chest. It was part of an old Ivan Turgenev collection she had picked up at the antique book shop near Boston Common. She had always been a big reader, but she couldn't breeze through action novels anymore. She hadn't even tried a mystery since Vinny kidnapped her. She stuck mostly to works by dead authors from centuries past. During her first semester of college, she had lived through more suspense than she had ever experienced from a thriller. She wondered if she'd ever be able to pick one up again. How had she once considered that kind of reading enjoyable?

"Hey there."

She recognized her lab partner's slightly accented voice, but her body still jumped.

"I'm sorry." Reuben frowned. "Are you all right?"

Kennedy let out her breath and didn't bother to blush. Not in front of Reuben. He had seen her at her worst this semester — he had seen her *through* her worst, really. She gave her best attempt at a smile. "I'm fine. Just a little anxious about the final."

Reuben glanced at her book. "I thought you were done with Russian lit for the semester."

Kennedy followed him into the lecture hall. "I am. I just brought this with me to read when everything's done."

Reuben snatched the volume out of her hands. "Actually, you're not going to have time for that."

Kennedy focused on grabbing it back so she didn't have to acknowledge the crowded, noisy lecture hall, with its endless rows of chairs, the perfect place for a kidnapper to blend in with the crowd. Professor Adell wouldn't be able to tell who was and who wasn't actually enrolled. If Vinny wanted, he could sit hunched over behind a test for the whole period, wait for Kennedy to finish, follow her out of the science building ...

After she was kidnapped that fall, her dad signed her up for a self-defense course, but Kennedy had done what she could to get out of it. She had been preparing for midterms by then, still struggling to make up the work she missed while recovering from her injuries. She didn't want the constant reminder of her own hopelessness, the powerlessness she felt while cuffed downstairs in that cold basement. She promised her dad she would enroll in the class during spring semester, but his message was as clear as an Erlenmeyer flask: Take self-defense, pass the course, or else fly back to China. He also ordered her some pepper spray, which he expected her to carry around wherever she went, even to the dorm bathroom and back.

At first, she tried to write her dad off as paranoid. But when Detective Drisklay started talking about security measures and even mentioned the possibility of witness protection, she realized how dangerous it was to have survived an attempted murder while one of the culprits was still at large. What could she do, though? Her self-defense course did more to creep her out than to instill confidence. The class focused on warding off one unarmed attacker. If or when Vinny came after her, it wouldn't be that simple.

"… celebrate the end of the semester," Reuben was saying.

Kennedy's head felt as though it was spinning, an electron buzzing around the nucleus in its nebulous cloud orbital, constantly in motion. Constantly searching for the perfect energy level, still rushing around madly after finding it.

"That sounds great." Kennedy wondered what she had agreed to.

"Where are you going?" Reuben asked. Kennedy loved his clipped Kenyan accent, but now she could barely hear it over the drone of so many dozens of students waiting to take their final exam, waiting to see which of them would pass on to next semester and which would become one of the leagues of Harvard pre-med dropouts. So much noise. So much bustle. Enough to drown out a muffled scream or the shot of Vinny's gun.

Kennedy slipped into an aisle desk near the back of the room. Reuben stared down at her. "Why all the way back here?"

Kennedy and Reuben had spent their semester in this lecture hall in the two center seats of row three, but now when she looked at their usual place, all she could think about was how many students would fill up behind her, students she couldn't see. Students she didn't know.

She shrugged. "I thought it might be nice to be in the back today, you know, just so we can be that much closer to the exit when we're done."

"We'll still have to walk to the front to hand in our papers."

Kennedy didn't respond but swung her knees to the side so Reuben could slip in beside her. He passed her a stick of gum. "Hey, if I get stuck on a problem, can I take a peek at yours?"

Kennedy chuckled. She and Reuben were both getting good grades, but he managed to do so without giving himself an ulcer. While Kennedy recovered from her injuries after her kidnapping last fall, Reuben had been there, talking her through the lectures she missed, encouraging her through the quizzes she had to make up.

He leaned toward her. "Just remember, nothing can be harder than that calculus final yesterday."

Kennedy didn't even want to think about it. She had one focus now. Finishing chemistry. The very last exam before semester break. It didn't matter that Vinny had tried to kill her less than two months earlier. It didn't matter that he had evaded Detective Drisklay and the scores of police officers searching for him. It didn't matter that her parents were working in China and couldn't afford to fly Kennedy home for Christmas. It didn't matter that she would be lucky if she passed yesterday's calculus test with a B. All that mattered was that in an hour and a half her last final would be over. She still had laundry to wash. She still had clothes to pack. And there was that meeting with Detective Drisklay in the morning before she left for her aunt's. But she didn't need to worry about any of that right now. She had excelled in chemistry this semester, even more than in her AP class in high school back in Yanji. This was her day to outshine even her own high expectations.

Professor Adell stood in front of the room. She was an eccentric old woman. Some whispered she was one of the few remaining Holocaust survivors; others said her parents immigrated and she was born after the war ended. Nobody quite knew how she had gotten so involved in chemistry, but it was impossible to deny she had found her passion. After filling up the chalkboard with notes during her lectures, instead of pausing to erase the whole thing, she would throw the eraser into her right hand and switch to writing with her left. Her students couldn't tell if she was originally right- or left-handed; the writing was atrocious either way.

She was a great scientist and decent lecturer, but not much of a motivational speaker. "Take your tests. Turn them in when you're done. No noise." Those were Professor Adell's only instructions, and she passed the exams out to the students in the front. Kennedy stared at the back of everyone's heads. Was someone here who shouldn't be? Someone who had sneaked in just to watch Kennedy, make sure she didn't leave the science building alive?

The stack of chemistry finals eventually made it to Kennedy and Reuben in the back of the hall.

"Good luck," Reuben whispered, clicking the back of his mechanical pencil.

She pried her eyes away from the other students. She had to focus. She took a deep breath and skimmed the problems on the first page. She could do this. It would be fine.

A tickle in the back of her throat. Was she catching a cold? No, she couldn't get sick. She was flying to Baltimore tomorrow to spend Christmas with her aunt. It wasn't the same as going home to her parents in Yanji, but at least she'd be out of the Boston area. Vinny couldn't reach her there, could he? Of course, he could hack into the Logan Airport system, look up her flight plans …

No, she couldn't think like that. She had a test. A test she was supposed to ace. That's all that mattered. There were a hundred people here. She was safe.

She cleared her throat, and another student a few rows ahead coughed back at her. She licked her lips, felt Reuben's glance, and attacked the first problem.

She was halfway through the second page when it came again. That tickle. Why hadn't she thought to bring a water bottle? Or a cough drop? She tore off a corner of her test and spit out her gum. She let out three coughs, loud enough for Professor Adell to frown at her from the front of the lecture hall.

A nice deep breath. That's all she needed. But when she tried, her lungs refused to expand and convulsed instead. More stares. She coughed again.

Reuben turned his head. "Are you ok?"

"I just need a drink," Kennedy whispered, and a student in the middle of the room let out a loud, "*Shhhhhh.*" Kennedy raised her hand, but Professor Adell was already glaring at her. Kennedy pointed to the back doors. The drinking fountains were just around the corner. Couldn't she run and come right back? Adell took a few seconds to respond. Did she think that Kennedy was going to cheat? That she had stashed some formula or answer sheet outside the lecture hall? If she had wanted to do something like that, she could have just brought it with her to the test. Who would notice one dishonest student out of so many?

Finally, Adell gave a curt nod, and Kennedy slipped out of her chair, thankful she was near the back. She knew Reuben was watching, probably worrying about her, but before she could give him a reassuring smile, another coughing fit seized her, and she ran up the stairs trying to stifle it.

In the hallway, she coughed so hard she thought she'd throw up. Doubled over, hacking on the floor, she pictured the young girl who had been kidnapped with her. Hopelessness wrapped its unyielding, icy tentacles around Kennedy's body. She couldn't stop the coughing, just like she hadn't been able to stop the bleeding in that ice-cold basement. Helpless. Victimized. Paralyzed.

She still had to finish her test. She couldn't let her mind sink to these depths. She would pray. She would find a way to take these thoughts captive. She was shaking now. Her whole body was trembling, reminding her of the pit bull who lived next door to her growing up who would thrash his head and growl until Kennedy ran home in tears and hysterics to her mother's arms.

She stumbled to the drinking fountain and waited for her breathing to calm down. The first attempt at a drink failed and sent snot-flavored juices burning her sinuses. By the third try she could manage a few sips. She didn't dare a deep inhale, but she could take a few short breaths before she had to cough again.

This was ridiculous. She had a final to finish. Her last test of the semester. If she didn't get back to the lecture hall soon, Adell really would accuse her of cheating.

She just needed to pray more. Isn't that what Christians always said? You're in trouble? Pray about it. Your parents are so busy training underground missionaries they don't even care that you brought home another straight-A report card? Pray about it. You're ready to take your last final of the semester, but a horrible cough has got you trapped outside in the hall because you know the moment you walk in you're going to become one gasping, wheezing, hacking mess?

Pray about it.

Well, Kennedy did pray. In fact, she had been praying all semester, at least since she got back to campus after her kidnapping. Praying for relief from the nightmares. Praying for the scar on her back not to stand out so glaringly on her pale skin. Praying for her body to stop trembling at random times, interrupting her studies, flashing her back to that cold, dark basement.

By now, Kennedy was all out of prayer energy.

Besides, didn't God know what she needed before she even asked? Didn't he see how needy she was right now?

Pray about it. So simple to say. So hard when you actually have to pick up one boot and plant it in front of you. So hard when you've got to pull yourself out of murky water so deep you can't even see the bottom, so muddy you're stuck before you realize you're sinking one deadly centimeter at a time. The suffocating, soul-starving fear that grips you in the middle of the night when you should be asleep but wake up gasping, drenched in sweat and certain your assailant is staring into your second-story window, waiting until you drift off to sleep again before he finishes you off for good. That's what Kennedy had been trying to pray against, but it was like trying to send a rainstorm back up to the troposphere with a broken umbrella.

She pulled back some of the hair that had fallen out of her ponytail and counted. Five seconds since her last cough. Maybe she was ready now. She had been accepted out of high school into Harvard's early-admissions medical program, but that offer was contingent on her GPA. If she failed general chemistry, even with high scores in all her other classes, she would probably end up on academic probation. Maybe even flunk out of the pre-med program altogether.

The itch tickled its way up her throat once more, and Kennedy decided she'd take another sip from the fountain and then go back. Until she threw up or got thrown out of the lecture hall for distracting other students, she would finish that final, and she would get the A she had worked for all semester, the A she deserved.

A door opened, and for a moment Kennedy worried some cocky TA would come out and shush her for making so much noise in the hall, but all Kennedy saw was a bald head and two mean, brooding eyes that widened as soon as they met hers. The door shut. The face disappeared. Kennedy's stomach dropped to the floor of her abdominal cavity.

She would have recognized that face anywhere.

Vinny.

CHAPTER 2

This was no time for her body to give out. Her heart pounded in her chest like the horrible thumping in that Edgar Allen Poe story, and her legs propelled her past the drinking fountain and out of the science center before she realized her coughing had stopped. Her boots pounded on the pavement, their echoes crashing in her ears. Could she hear Vinny behind her? Would he chase her, or would he just gun her down? Zigzag. Shouldn't she run in a zigzag? Somewhere in her dad's crazy crisis training, didn't he say something about it being easiest to shoot someone if they were running in a straight line?

But what if Vinny was coming after her on foot? She didn't have time to waste on cute little twists and curves and slithering snake patterns. She had to get somewhere safe. She couldn't slow down. She had to get to shelter. If Vinny had a gun, would she hear it and then feel the hot fiery pain in her back? Or would it happen all at once? Was there really such a thing as dying instantly like the police reports claimed? Could you ever die so quickly you didn't even realize what had happened?

Ahead of her, someone unlocked the dorm. Just a little more exertion, and she could reach it before the door closed. "Hold it!" she tried to yell, but she was going so fast her voice got lost somewhere behind her.

The door shut just as Kennedy slammed into it. She didn't take the time to look back. Vinny would be on her any second.

Someone opened the dorm from the inside, and she darted in, not even pausing to glance at her savior or mumbling, "Excuse me."

Up the stairs, two by two, hoisting herself up with the handrail when her thigh muscles got too tired. *Please let Willow be in. Please let Willow be in*, her mind begged, and she strained to see down the hall. Was the door open just a little? That would save at least twenty seconds if she didn't have to stop and fiddle with her keys.

Please be open. Please be open.

Yes!

Kennedy pushed through the door, slammed it shut behind her, and threw back the deadbolt. She jumped to her roommate's side of the room just in case Vinny shot straight through the door.

The police. She had to call the police. She reached around for her backpack. It wasn't on her shoulders. She had left it in the science hall. She needed a phone. Where was Willow's?

At that point, Kennedy first noticed her roommate staring at her from her bed. Under the covers beside her was someone Kennedy had never met. At the beginning of the semester, she might have been surprised, but right now she didn't care what Willow was doing or who she was doing it with. She just had to let the police know Vinny was after her.

"I need your phone."

Willow raised an eyebrow.

"I'm sorry," Kennedy panted. "It's an emergency. And ..." She turned her back. "Well, sorry for barging in."

Willow swept her blanket off. "Don't worry. We're still decent."

Over the course of the semester, Kennedy had grown to enjoy Willow and her carefree style, but right now she needed someone whose brain functioned faster than a viscous gelatin. "I just saw Vinny," she panted. "I need your phone."

Any minute, Kennedy expected to hear Vinny pounding on the door outside. She wondered how much damage she'd do to Willow's computer if she slid it and the whole desk against the door as a barricade. Why was Willow just reclining there with that dazed, questioning expression? Didn't she realize Kennedy was the one person Vinny wanted dead more than anyone else?

"Where is your phone?" she panted.

"You say you saw Vinny?" Willow's voice was softer than normal. Subdued. Almost gentle.

"I ran all the way here." For just a minute, confusion mingled with the acidic fear that raged and foamed in Kennedy's stomach. "He was right behind me."

Willow stood up. Slowly. As if she was afraid of hurting Kennedy if she moved too fast. She reached out her bejeweled hand. Softly squeezed Kennedy's shoulder with those long, painted nails. "That cute journalist you'd been talking to stopped by this morning. You know, the ginger?" Willow stared at the wall behind Kennedy and took a deep breath. "He wanted to ask if you'd heard the news. Vinny's been in custody since last night."

CHAPTER 3

Adrenaline oozed out of Kennedy's pores. She sank down in Willow's chair.

"You sure?"

Willow twirled a strand of her wavy hair around her finger. "Yeah. I thought about texting you, but I didn't know if you'd get too distracted from your finals."

Kennedy sat up a little taller. "Well, he must have escaped or something. He must have gotten out and come here and …"

Willow leaned over to her computer and went to Channel 2's website. She pointed at the man whose face was plastered on the home screen under the headline *Kidnapping Suspect Caught in North End.* "This him?"

Kennedy glanced at the picture. "Yeah." Her legs wobbled, and she turned away.

Willow scrolled down. "He's most definitely still in jail."

Kennedy slouched down and swallowed. Why did she

feel like crying? This should be good news. It should be great news, except for the fact that she just ran a quarter of a mile from a phantom. A bald nothing.

"Hey, maybe you should go."

For a minute, Kennedy thought Willow was talking to her. She had forgotten about the boy in the bed.

"No prob." He got up and tucked his shirt into his pants. "Call you tonight?"

Willow kept her eyes on the computer screen. "Nah, I'm going to Cape Cod with some buddies for a few days."

"Maybe after that?"

His voice was hopeful, but Willow still didn't look up. "Yeah, happy Hanukkah. Or Christmas. Or whatever."

Willow's friend gave Kennedy a slightly apologetic glance, unlocked the door, and headed out.

Kennedy stared at her lap. "Sorry for ruining your date."

Willow clicked off her monitor. "Don't worry about it. Seriously. He had wicked bad breath."

Kennedy laughed but knew it sounded forced and artificial. "I really don't know what happened. I seriously thought ..."

Willow flicked her wrist as if swatting the rest of Kennedy's apology away. "You don't need to say anything.

You had a horrible semester. You got kidnapped, watched some little girl nearly bleed to death, had a crazy dude with a knife ..."

"I get it."

"Anyway ..." Willow stared at herself in the little mirror on her desk and adjusted her hand-crafted earrings. "At least your imaginary friend waited to show up until you were done with your final, right?"

Kennedy blinked.

"You were finished with the test before you did your little sprint in those cute boots, right?"

Kennedy shook her head.

"Hey, it's ok." Willow sounded like she was talking to a puppy with a hurt paw. "You can always explain to your professor what happened. With everything you've been through ..."

How could Kennedy have been so stupid? Didn't she know Vinny wouldn't dare risk showing himself in broad daylight in a building full of witnesses? Why had she run? And how many people saw her acting like the fool she was?

"It's all right," Willow repeated.

What should she do? She couldn't go back to the lecture hall and expect to pick up right where she left off. The test started over half an hour ago. Even if the professor let her back in to finish her exam, it didn't seem fair to the other students, and there was no way to explain the circumstances to Adell without distracting the entire room. Besides, Kennedy was tired of all the publicity. Her image had been splashed all over the news last fall, and even now she could almost hear the thoughts of people who stared at her a second too long: *That's the one who got kidnapped. That's the one they got with that little pregnant girl.* She didn't need to rehash the entire scenario. She needed to move on.

Forgetting what is behind, straining toward what was ahead. Wasn't that how the Bible verse went? She had been trying to memorize Scripture lately, Scripture she could turn to whenever she recalled Vinny's face, the feel of the unforgiving handcuff biting her wrist. She had spent so much mental energy over the past six weeks convincing her parents she was fine. If only she could reach the place where she believed it. Where was the victory Pastor Carl talked about in his sermons? Where was the freedom, the dramatic deliverance from fear and the nightmares that plagued her?

"... cute lab partner of yours?" Willow's voice interrupted Kennedy's thoughts, and she tried to recreate the entire sentence.

"What about him?"

Willow let out a dramatic huff. "I said, would you be more comfortable explaining it to the professor if he came with you?"

Kennedy went to her own desk and turned on her computer. It was nice of Willow to try to help, but her suggestions were about as effective as salt dumped into a solution when it's already past its saturation point.

"I'll just email Adell," she replied. "See what she says."

"Don't forget to play the whole I-was-kidnapped card. If I were you, I'd be milking that for all it's worth, and I'd have signed for that book deal, too."

Ignoring Willow's remarks, Kennedy let her computer start up. Adell would understand, right? She'd let Kennedy take the test tonight. Or first thing tomorrow before she met with Detective Drisklay. Maybe Willow had a point. After everything Kennedy had gone through, a little slack wasn't too much to ask for, was it?

Willow came up behind and rubbed Kennedy's back. "You sure you don't want to come with us to the Cape? Might help you relax a little. Get some of that tension out of your neck."

She started massaging the deep muscle, and Kennedy cringed.

"You are so tight up here." Willow dug in even deeper. "It's like your neck has turned into the dumping grounds for every single negative emotion in your body."

Kennedy turned around to face her. "You don't need to worry about me. I'm all right."

Willow raised her eyebrows. "Really? Well, I still think you should come with me. You should see the cabin we got. It's wicked posh. We have room in the car for one more."

Willow made for a good roommate and even a decent friend, but her crowd of noisy, boisterous theater majors made Kennedy feel like a drop of oil floating in isolation in a lava lamp. She mumbled something about meeting with the detective in the morning and went back to typing her apology to Professor Adell.

Kennedy stared at her half-composed email and glanced at the time. The test would probably go for another half an hour, maybe more. She could go back and finish it right now if she had the chance. Why had she let her imagination play such a horrid trick on her?

She reread her email but still wasn't happy with the finished product. She deleted everything she wrote about running away from Vinny and just said she had been coughing too much and didn't want to disturb the class.

How would Adell react? Would she think Kennedy was just trying to get out of her work?

Well, there was nothing else she could do. Not right now. Except maybe start that laundry and pack for Aunt Lilian's. It would be a short hop to Baltimore, nothing like the flight between China and the States. She could take one or two volumes of her antique Turgenev set to read on the plane. She just hoped it'd be enough to keep her mind off everything else. *Forget what's behind. Strain toward what's ahead.* If she could block out her memories from last fall, that basement, everything would be fine. She could live that victorious Christian life she heard everyone talk about. She could even be a witness, a living example of how God helps people overcome adversity. If she weren't petrified by public speaking, she could even become a motivational speaker. *If God can bring me through a kidnapping and attempted murder, he can carry you through whatever problems you're dealing with today.*

If only she could bring herself to believe it.

"Well, I've gotta get going." Willow leaned down and pecked the air by Kennedy's cheek. "Promise me you'll relax a little, ok? Especially with them catching Vinny and all. I mean, that's really good news. Oh, and get in touch with that reporter. He's cute." Willow picked up her bag and glided out, leaving the door a crack open behind her.

Kennedy's heart dropped slowly, like crystallized honey sinking in a cup of tea. After a brainless eternity staring at her computer, she got up and gathered her laundry into a heap. There was so much to do before she flew out. Why had she let it pile up this high?

A couple of minutes later, the computer dinged at her, and she glanced at her screen. Professor Adell had already replied.

Medical excuses may be permitted at the discretion of the professor provided a note from the campus medical center verifies the necessity of said provision.

That was all, no names or greetings or *hope you're feeling better.* Not even an automatic closing or signature at the bottom. Kennedy reread it, each time wishing for more information. She hadn't ever been to the campus medical center. She didn't know if she needed to bring her parents' insurance card or write a check or what. And how much would it cost? She had spent most of her discretionary funds at the used bookstore downtown. Well, it was either visit the clinic or fail the final. Maybe she could conjure up another coughing fit for the doctor or nurse and get a quick excuse. Why couldn't she be like Willow? Her roommate could probably convince someone she was dying of meningitis to get out of a test.

Kennedy buttoned up her new leather coat, an early Christmas gift from her dad, checked Harvard's webpage to remember where she was supposed to go, and headed to the medical center.

CHAPTER 4

Kennedy opened her mouth for the middle-aged doctor in his white lab coat. She stared at his little flashlight and performed all the other tests he doled out. She didn't have to overact to make her movements slow and lazy. As soon as she got out from the wind and sat down in the clinic, exhaustion clung to each individual ligament like hoarfrost.

"You said your throat's been hurting?" He frowned, and Kennedy felt about as nervous as she had been during her phone interview with Harvard Medical School's curly admissions application committee.

"It's a little better now, I guess. It was just during the test. I kept coughing, so I went into the hall to get a drink, and it got worse."

He nodded his head slowly and studied Kennedy over his glasses.

"Then I went back to my room." Why had she told him that? He didn't react, and she didn't have any choice now but to go on. "And, well, it got a little better then."

"And then you came here?" he asked. "For what? A prescription?"

"I started to worry I might have strep," Kennedy recited the little white lie she had formed on the way over. "I'm supposed to fly to my aunt's tomorrow, down to Baltimore, and, well, I thought maybe I should get checked out before I went on a plane." She squirmed, wondering how many germs were on the table bed where she sat.

He kept his pen poised over his clipboard but didn't write anything. "And how did your test go? Did your coughing interfere with your final?"

Kennedy tried to meet his eyes, but her gaze settled somewhere near his salt and pepper mustache. "Well, I started coughing right in the middle. It was hard to breathe, and I didn't want to disrupt anyone, and, well, I just left my paper there."

"So you're looking for a medical excuse?" His voice was steady and somewhat bored, but Kennedy felt her palms clam up.

"I told the professor I'd be willing to retake it."

He frowned. "I see ..." He glanced down at his clipboard. "Kennedy." He paused, and she knew from his furrowed brow what was coming next. "Kennedy Stern. Where have I heard that name before?"

She stared at her lap, wondering if he'd come to the realization on his own or if she'd have to jog his memory.

"Kennedy Stern," he repeated. "Aren't you the girl who was ..."

He paused, leaving Kennedy to finish on his behalf. "Kidnapped."

He nodded. "Well, I'm glad you're back safe and unharmed."

There was that tickle again. Was she going to have another coughing attack here?

"You say you had a hard time breathing. Has that happened to you before?"

"No, not that I can ..." Kennedy stopped.

Guilt must have been etched on her face, because the doctor leaned toward her. "Yes?"

She sighed. "Well, there was one time. A few weeks after I was ... after I got back to campus." She glanced up to make sure he understood. He nodded, so she continued. "I thought I saw someone in the student union. Turns out it was nothing, at least I think it was. But I started running, and I was coughing then, too. Had a hard time catching my breath again."

She didn't mention the tears. The sobbing that convinced her she was on the verge of hyperventilating.

She didn't mention barging into her dorm room in the middle of Willow's make-out session with a student from the theater department. Kennedy's mortification snapped her out of her panic, but thankfully her roommate wasn't upset. "He was really sweaty and gross, anyway," she insisted. A little while later, once Kennedy stopped trembling, Willow suggested, "Maybe you should see a shrink or something."

Kennedy had shoved the suggestion aside. After all, she was a Christian. She needed to pray more, that's what she needed to do, not talk out her trauma with a therapist who would stretch her out on a couch and make her relive those twenty-four hours all over again. She forced herself to focus once more on her schoolwork, carried her pepper spray wherever she went for the next week, and did a decent job of forgetting about the whole cafeteria episode. Still, she didn't eat any hot meals for a while and subsisted on dry Cheerios, Craisins, and microwave popcorn until she could enter the student union without shaking.

None of that had anything to do with getting a medical excuse to Professor Adell, though, so she shrugged. "That's all."

The doctor didn't look convinced, but he mercifully didn't press the issue. "So you had a hard time breathing this afternoon. And coughing?"

She nodded. Hadn't she just told him that?

"Wheezing?" he asked.

"No." She didn't mention the gasping. That was easily enough explained because of how fast she had been running.

"Any other changes?" he asked, finally looking up at her. "Heart rate? Chills? Drop or increase in body temperature?"

"I don't know." More frustration crept into Kennedy's voice than she had intended. It's not like she had stopped sprinting to check her vitals.

He pursed his lips and squinted while he scribbled on his pad. "I'll email your professor a medical excuse. When did you say you fly out?"

"Tomorrow." Kennedy wondered why it felt like she was back in high school and he was writing her a detention slip.

"Well, then, within your first week on campus next semester, I want you to make an appointment with one of our therapists. I'm writing you a prescription for counseling right now."

"Counseling?" Couldn't he have handed her a bag of cough drops, given her a note for Adell, and wished her happy holidays?

He ripped the page noisily off its pad and handed her the slip. His handwriting was large and scrawling, nearly as sloppy as Professor Adell's, but the largest words right in the middle of the page were as clear as a beaker.

Post-traumatic stress disorder.

"That's not an official diagnosis," he explained. "But after what you've been through, it's worth ruling out."

Kennedy's throat constricted.

"You've had a rough semester." He glanced at her meaningfully. "That's nothing to be ashamed of."

"I'm not ..." Kennedy began but stopped. If she tried defending herself, she'd look even guiltier. She forced a smile. "Thank you."

He answered with a half-smile of his own, and she walked out the room, conscious of his eyes on her. How did normal people walk, those without PTSD? Could he tell if she was infected just by her gait? She wasn't sick. She wasn't stressed. Well, no more stressed than usual. And besides, it was finals week. Who wasn't anxious, at least just a little?

The sun wasn't setting yet, but the sky was that shade of grayish pink only seen in winter as Kennedy trudged back to her dorm. She would rather have made up the final first thing in the morning. Counseling? Was he serious? *Give a quack a white coat, and he thinks he can read souls all of a sudden.* Kennedy was a Christian. She didn't get traumatized. Worried, maybe. Stressed, for sure. But full-scale trauma? That was for POWs and war veterans and all those firemen who saw thousands die the day the Twin Towers fell. Not girls like her. No, Kennedy had the Bible, and she had prayer. Maybe she just hadn't been trying hard enough. She gripped the prescription slip, braced herself against the biting wind, and hurried to her dorm.

She stomped up the stairs, certain all she needed was a night of solitude. A night without Willow and the ridiculously dramatized shouts and cursing from those silly shooter video games her roommate always played. A night without worrying about homework or lab papers or due dates. A night just to herself, just her books, her fuzzy pink bathrobe, some hot chocolate, and …

"So there you are!"

She recognized Reuben's voice and took a moment to collect herself before turning around on the staircase.

"I've been looking all over for you." He held up her backpack. "You forgot this."

She was glad he didn't ask specifically about the test. She didn't want to think about it. "I, um, I went to see the doctor about my cough." She crumpled the paper even more tightly in her fist.

"What did he say?"

They were at Kennedy's door by now, and Reuben stopped while Kennedy fidgeted with the lock. He followed her in without invitation and plopped down in Willow's beanbag chair.

"Well?"

Kennedy had already lost the progression of the conversation. "Well, what?"

"What did the doctor say? About the cough?"

She tossed the wad onto her desk. "Wants me to go to counseling. He thinks I have PTSD or something." She half expected to feel a warm surge of relief when the words were out, but all she could feel was the quivering in her abdomen and the hot sting of embarrassment.

Reuben didn't smile and didn't frown. He looked right into Kennedy's eyes far too long for comfort. "That's an interesting suggestion," he finally stated without emotion.

"Interesting?"

He cocked his head to the side. "Well, do you have any objections?"

The question caught her off guard. She had been prepared to defend herself if he said it was a good idea.

Instead, she had to rethink her arguments and failed to come up with anything coherent.

"It sounds to me like you're in need of some serious holiday cheer." He grabbed her scarf and held it out.

"What are you doing?"

"You and I are going off campus. We need to celebrate the end of the semester, the start of the Christmas season. With this." He reached into his back pocket and pulled out two tickets.

"*The Nutcracker*?"

"It's an American holiday tradition. And since this is my first Christmas in America, I decided we should go."

She wanted to smile. Wanted to laugh. Wanted to give him a hug to thank him for being that thoughtful. But she was so tired.

"Don't you like ballet?"

She couldn't bear to disappoint him. She wrapped the scarf around her neck and grabbed her book bag.

"The show doesn't start until seven." He grinned. "Which gives us just enough time to stop by Common Treasures and get you a few more books. What do you say?"

She was tired. Far more tired than she wanted to admit. But she wasn't traumatized. *Forgetting what is behind, straining toward what is ahead.* Forcing a smile, she followed Reuben out the door and checked the lock behind them. There was a lightness in her step she hadn't known in months. Maybe a night out was just what she needed.

CHAPTER 5

"What do you think of this one?"

Kennedy looked at the book Reuben held up. She loved the antique smell here, even though she figured the workers at Common Treasures Books were probably at risk for developing lung cancer or some other tragic malady from spending their time in the dust and mildew.

"*Catcher in the Rye*?" She frowned. "I read that once in tenth grade. Could barely understand it. Baseball and trains, right?"

Reuben chuckled. "Close. Except it was fencing."

"Oh, really?" Kennedy asked. "I could have sworn it was baseball."

"Well, there's the part where ..." Something else caught Reuben's eye, and he snatched another book off the shelf. "I loved this one!"

Kennedy gawked. "*Lord of the Flies*? Are you serious? That made me want to barf."

Reuben was already flipping through the pages,

thumbing back and forth, letting his eyes skim over the passages. "This was the very first book I read in English literature."

Kennedy had nothing to say and strolled around the bend to another section. Reuben followed reluctantly. She pointed to the spine of an old hardback copy of *Pride and Prejudice*. "You know, I never did get what all the hype was over Mr. Darcy. He was just a rich, eccentric introvert, but about half the girls in my high school had major literary crushes on him."

Reuben raised an eyebrow. "Really? I found the whole thing dry and hard to follow."

"It's not hard to follow." Kennedy was already scanning other titles on the shelf. "Oh, they have *Little Women*." She pulled out the book. "You know, I think my grandma gave me an edition with these same illustrations. I wonder what I did with it."

Reuben opened the front cover and pointed at the price penciled in the top corner. "You should find it. That's enough to pay for next semester's textbooks."

Kennedy gently placed the volume back on the shelf. "You know, this is one of the only two novels I've read that's actually made me mad."

Reuben checked the time and slipped his phone back

into his pocket. "Really? Why's that?"

"I just always thought Jo should have married Laurie. I was furious when she turned him down." She watched him button up his coat and asked, "Is it time to go?"

"Pretty soon. Show starts in twenty minutes."

Kennedy placed the book back on its shelf and bundled up. "Well, next time we come here, we need to find something that we've both read and we both like."

Reuben held the shop door open and nodded at the owner. "We might be here for days if we tried that."

The wind had picked up, and Kennedy tucked her scarf into her leather jacket to keep it from flapping in her face. She increased her pace. They hadn't spent very long at the bookshop, but it was the first time in weeks she hadn't thought about classwork or finals or kidnappers or anything horrible like that. The campus doctor didn't know what he was talking about. She didn't need therapy. She just needed a chance to relax.

The Opera House was only two blocks away from Common Treasures, so they walked instead of taking the T. Kennedy asked Reuben how he spent Christmas in Kenya, but the wind was howling so loud she had to stand practically shoulder to shoulder and hip to hip with him to hear his response.

"We'd always go up country to my grandfather's farm." He shrugged. "It wasn't all that different from family gatherings here, I assume. We walked to church on Christmas Eve. Didn't get home until after midnight. On Christmas Day, my grandfather's first wife would butcher one of the cows, and then we'd all ..."

"You butchered a whole cow?" Kennedy recalled how much of a fuss her mom made over a fifteen-pound turkey.

"Well, I didn't. Grandmother did."

"How did your family go through that much meat?" Kennedy didn't know if Kenyans "up country" would have freezers or even the electricity to run them. Reuben had talked a lot about growing up in the city, but this was the first time he had mentioned anything outside Nairobi.

Reuben laughed. "You'd be surprised at how fast a hundred people can eat a cow."

Kennedy leaned forward. "Did you say a hundred?"

"Around there. It changes each year depending on who's gotten married, who's had a new baby, and who's passed away."

Kennedy thought back to the largest family gathering she could remember. It was probably her grandma's funeral. The wake was for relatives only, and she guessed there were twenty people there, certainly no more. Before she moved to Yanji, getting together with "family" usually meant her grandma, Aunt Lilian, Uncle Jack, and sometimes Uncle Jack's two teenagers who spent every other holiday with him. Kennedy had figured it out once when she was younger. They were her step-cousins-in-law, and once Aunt Lilian and Uncle Jack split up, she had to tack an *ex* to the front of that and make the title longer and more confusing. She hadn't seen them in over a decade and couldn't remember the older boy's name anymore. Still, they were the closest thing Kennedy had to extended family around her own age.

"So where do a hundred people sleep?" she asked, thinking about how uncomfortable Aunt Lilian's roll-away trundle bed was.

"Wherever we can."

Kennedy's mind was reeling, like water molecules zipping around in a steaming pot. "I still can't imagine having that many cousins. How many aunts and uncles do you have?"

Reuben furrowed his brow. "I'm not sure. I counted once, but I probably forgot a few."

"Well," Kennedy tried again, "how many kids did your grandparents have?"

"Twenty-three."

Kennedy's eyes grew as wide as the pipette bulbs in her chemistry lab. "Your poor grandma!"

Reuben laughed. "Well, that number was spread out over three wives."

"Three? That's a lot of times to be widowed."

"No, three at the same time. They're all still alive. It wasn't all that unheard of back in his day, you know."

"Really? They still do that there?"

"Not so much anymore, but yeah, in the past it was common." Reuben's voice had grown even softer, so Kennedy could hardly hear him over the wind.

"Will it be hard for you not going back this year?" she asked.

He looked away. Quickened his pace. "It wouldn't be the same even if I went back now."

A heaviness clouded the air between them like fog in a beaker. She had known Reuben long enough to recognize these brooding moods of his. She forced false enthusiasm into her voice. "Well, it's like I already told you, if you don't want to spend Christmas by yourself, I'm sure my pastor and his wife would love to …"

"Thanks, but it's fine. Really. Here we are." Reuben was apparently ready to end their conversation as soon as they arrived at the Opera House, and Kennedy didn't press matters. They passed through the line and joined the other *Nutcracker* enthusiasts filing in to find their places.

"I thought it would be more crowded in here," Reuben stated as an usher led them to their seats in the highest balcony.

Kennedy was glad to hear him sounding more like himself. He could never stay very serious for more than a few minutes. She stared down at the hundreds of empty chairs below. "Maybe everyone's running late. That wind is awful."

Reuben leaned forward, his eyes wide.

"Do they have shows like this in Kenya?" she asked.

He didn't seem to hear her question over the sound of the tuning orchestra. "Look down there!" He pointed. "I think I just saw one of the dancers when the usher opened that door."

Kennedy hadn't seen anything. "That's probably the entrance to backstage or something."

"I wonder if we could go in there."

Before long, the lights dimmed, and Reuben finally sat in his seat. His right leg bounced like pressurized carbonation in a jar of soda. Kennedy was glad they were this high up or else he might have run right onstage in his enthusiasm. She had never cared all that much for *The*

Nutcracker. She had seen it a few times in Manhattan before her family moved to China, but it had never really enthralled her. Still, she was glad to be here with Reuben, glad to get her mind off everything that had plagued her recently.

When the orchestra began its first strain, Reuben sucked in his breath. She had to smile. As much time as the two of them had spent together over the past semester, she had never considered him the type to love ballet so much.

The first colorful dancers graced the stage, and he was completely lost. Sometimes she caught him keeping beat with one hand as if he were an assistant conductor. During the nutcracker's fight with the Rat King, Reuben leaned forward in his chair so far she was afraid he might topple right off the balcony. As soon as the curtain closed for intermission, even before the lights came on, he sprang to his feet. "Let's go!"

"What are you doing?"

He grabbed her hand and plucked up both their coats. "There's empty seats down there. I want to see everything closer."

On a normal night, Kennedy would have protested. She would have brought up issues like ticket prices and cranky ushers and would have forced Reuben to see reason. But his enthusiasm was catching. Besides, this was her night to throw worry to the wind and let it blow away into the Charles River, never to bother her again. They raced down the plush staircases to the lower level. A white-haired usher gave them both a quizzical look but didn't say anything when they scurried down the aisle.

"How close were you planning to go?" Kennedy whispered as Reuben rushed toward the front.

"As close as we can." He stared for a minute, paused, and squinted at the rows. "Over here," he finally said. "This area was pretty empty."

"Are you sure nobody was here?" Kennedy asked as he set his coat down on one of the chairs in the fourth row.

"If someone was, we'll just say we forgot where we were and move somewhere else. No problem."

Kennedy wanted to protest, but Reuben wasn't even looking at her anymore. He was staring straight up at the huge dome ceiling, with all the graceful cherubs and dancers frolicking in the painted clouds.

"I've seen some beautiful things back home," he breathed, "but not like this."

Kennedy had to admit it was gorgeous. If it hadn't been for Reuben, would she even have thought to look up?

"So, are you having a good time?" he asked.

Kennedy set her leather coat across the back of her chair. "Yeah." She took in a deep breath, thankful she hadn't had a single coughing fit since her exam.

The lights dimmed, the hum of conversation died down, and the sounds of the orchestra softly tuning their instruments billowed out to Reuben and Kennedy's new seats. Thankfully, nobody pestered them for their chairs, and none of the ushers seemed to notice or care that they had slipped so close to the front even though they only carried cheap student tickets. Reuben's leg bounced even more quickly when the curtain opened and revealed the ground fog and majestic backdrop of the Land of Sweets. For the entire second act, during the parts where she might have been tempted to lose herself in daydreams, Kennedy just glanced over at Reuben, saw his enraptured expression in the dim lights from the stage, and decided this was a perfect evening out.

Now that she thought about it, this was the first time she and Reuben had been off campus together without their textbooks and lab assignments in tow. She couldn't even remember a meal in the student union with him that didn't consist of at least some degree of studying. Had she really been so serious all semester? Layer after layer of exhaustion and anxiety lifted off her shoulders as she sat, mesmerized and enchanted just like Clara beside the prince.

When the curtain closed, Reuben clapped so loud it shot vicarious pain to Kennedy's palms. He didn't say anything as they got their coats and worked their way back to the aisle. Kennedy was about to follow the crowds out the main doors, but Reuben took her by the elbow.

"Wait a minute. I want to see something."

She hesitated before he dragged her to the side door he had spotted from the balcony. A short, stocky usher with spectacles scowled a few feet in front of it. He had a clipboard in his hand and was talking to two well-dressed adults. After a minute, he put his hand to his earpiece and then waved the patrons through.

"Back here," Reuben whispered. "Just act like you know what you're doing." Bypassing a few others who had formed a short line, he slipped in behind the two going through, and Kennedy followed, expecting any minute to hear the angry protests of the old man.

The door shut behind them.

"We made it." He tightened his hold on her arm.

Kennedy didn't know whether to laugh or chide him. "I can't believe you actually did that."

He ran, tugging her down a set of stairs to a hallway and down a small side corridor, giggling like a guilty child.

47

"Come on." Reuben pulled her arm again. "I want to see if we can meet some of the dancers."

"I really don't think we're supposed to ..." Kennedy stopped as a whole flock of little girls scurried past.

"Aren't those the ones who came out of that woman's dress?" Reuben waved at the ballerinas, who hardly noticed him. He ran down the next hall, and Kennedy followed behind, feeling lighter and more playful than she had in years. In all her time living in Yanji, had she ever done anything this spontaneous?

Reuben hurried straight ahead, but she thought she heard someone behind them. The near-sighted usher, maybe, ready to put an end to their mischief? She stopped and spun around, her heart gripped with foreboding. Nobody was there. She let out a sigh and turned back toward Reuben.

He was gone.

The hallway was infinitely narrower than she remembered it. Why did they keep the lights so bright down here? She had turned so many times she couldn't figure out where she was anymore in relation to the rest of the Opera House. Was this beneath the stage? There were no marked exits, no friendly old ladies with flashlights ready to show you the way. Where did Reuben go?

The tickle returned to the back of her throat. She hadn't thought to bring any cough drops. Not even a water bottle. Where had he run off to? Why hadn't he waited?

A chill covered her whole body although she was wearing her new coat. What if someone had followed them? What if they saw her go down beneath the Opera House? A sort of *Phantom-of-the-Opera*-type menace who would entrap her beneath the theater and hold her hostage in his cold, cement cell? Her wrists chaffed with the memory of handcuffs, and her lungs constricted without forcing out any air.

Where was Reuben? Had someone attacked him?

Her diaphragm spasmed. She couldn't inhale.

A door slammed shut. Was someone locking her in? Would she be stuck down here forever? Would anybody even know she was gone?

Help.

She slipped up to the wall for support. She couldn't hold herself up anymore. Had someone sucked all the air out from the basement?

Her cellphone. She could call Reuben. Call the police. Somebody would get her out of here. Somebody …

She fumbled through the zipper pockets of her backpack. Where was it?

Her fingers finally clenched the phone, which she had flipped off during the performance. She punched it on. Why did they take so long to start up again? A light flickered on the screen. A familiar, ominous tone.

No!

The batteries were low.

There was still enough power to make one call, wasn't there? *Please let there be enough.* She found Reuben's number in her contacts.

Please pick up.

Tiny bars danced across the screen. What was taking so long? She fought the urge to fling the phone to the ground. There wasn't enough reception down here.

Three short beeps, and then her screen flashed with the message: *Call failed.*

Fear jolted through her entire body. What if this was a setup?

"Kennedy?"

She jumped, flinging her bag around. It hit Reuben in the gut.

"Oof."

She forced herself to laugh, swallowing away the lump in her throat. "Don't scare me like that!" Did she sound like someone who had just been startled? Or did she sound like someone about to have a nervous breakdown?

"I'm sorry."

She sighed as her breath came back to her in a rush. "I didn't know where you went." She blinked her eyes. She had been taken aback, that was all. A little jolt. Nothing to worry about. Nothing to be ashamed of.

"I should have told you, but I thought you were behind me. Look. I just got a picture with the old guy. The uncle or grandfather or whoever he was." He showed her the picture. "Come on, I want to get one with both of us."

Kennedy shook her head. "You know, I'm actually getting really hungry. Do we have time to stop for something to eat?" Anything to get out of this basement.

"Angelo's Pizza?"

Kennedy forced excitement into her voice. "Perfect."

Reuben pointed. "I saw an exit back here. I think it goes right to the street level."

Kennedy followed a pace behind, squeezing back her hot and silent tears of shame.

CHAPTER 6

The wind whipped and howled around them when they emerged on a side street in back of the Opera House. Reuben stood a little in front and shielded Kennedy from the biting wind.

"That was so fun."

If Kennedy knew Reuben, he wouldn't stop gushing about the show until next semester.

He let out a contented sigh. "Ready for pizza?"

They made their way to the T station. Kennedy just wanted to get out of the cold. Loathing and humiliation clashed together in her gut. When would she stop acting like such a baby? Maybe she really was coming down with something.

Reuben hummed a little tune from *The Nutcracker* as they waited for the T, and Kennedy wondered what her friends from high school would say if they saw her today. At the All American Girls School in Yanji, she earned a reputation for being responsible and studious. Now, the same young woman who took four AP classes her senior year and still graduated as valedictorian couldn't sit through a simple general chemistry final without breaking down into a sobbing, coughing, hallucinating mess.

What was she doing wrong? She was praying. God knew how much she was praying these days. She had never been one for Bible study, at least not like the Secret Seminary students her parents trained in China, but for the past few weeks she had read her Bible nearly every morning and had memorized a dozen passages or more.

Forgetting what is behind, straining toward what is ahead. It sounded so simple. And if that's really what God wanted her to do, why hadn't he given her the ability to follow through? She was so busy on the weekends she didn't always make it to St. Margaret's Church, but she was there at least a few Sundays each month, and she went over to Pastor Carl and Sandy's for dinner a couple times, too. As far as she knew, she was doing everything right. By the book. Exactly what any Sunday school teacher or VBS leader would tell her. Prayer and Bible study were the keys to the victorious Christian life. So why was she floundering, flailing her arms and still sinking into the miry muck of anxiety? She couldn't remember the last time she had slept the whole night through. She didn't always remember her dreams, but she often woke up in the middle of the night drenched in sweat.

Dear God, what am I missing? I'm trying so hard.

"What are you thinking about?"

Kennedy had almost forgotten Reuben was still there and fumbled for a response. "Oh, I was just wondering if Professor Adell will want me to retake the test in the morning."

"I don't think you need to worry about your final. Even if you have to take it again, you'll do fine, like always."

The Green Line train pulled up to the platform. Kennedy didn't say anything else. Reuben followed her up the steps of the car, and they found seats toward the back.

Neither spoke as the subway chugged along noisily. When it came to the next stop, a heavyset woman in a huge fur coat climbed up the steps, panting from exertion. "Phew, that wind is really howling up there," she announced to nobody in particular. She caught Kennedy's eye and stared a few extra seconds before sitting across from her.

Another man came on, thickly built, slightly bald. His eyes passed over Kennedy, but he didn't smile. Had she seen him somewhere before?

"What will you be reading over break?" Reuben's voice

startled her, but she hid her surprise.

"I've still only made it through two of the Turgenev books." She glanced at the man, who was sitting near the emergency lever. He opened up a newspaper, and Kennedy looked away.

The fur coat lady still stared at her quizzically. Finally, she leaned forward. "Excuse me, but are you that girl from the news? The one that got kidnapped last fall?"

Kennedy's spine stiffened, and she wished those transporters from her dad's favorite sci-fi shows were real so she could beam herself straight to bed. Instead, she just gave a quick nod.

"I thought so." The woman folded her arms across her massive chest. "You know, I'm very good with faces. As soon as I saw you, I knew you had been on the news. Terrible thing, isn't it, what happened to that little girl?"

Reuben leaned over and whispered in her ear, "We can get on another train at the next stop if you want."

Kennedy shook her head. She was a gifted, mature, capable young woman. Isn't that what all of her high school teachers had written in their letters of recommendation to Harvard? What kind of straight-A pre-med student couldn't handle a little chitchat with a nosy stranger on the T?

"You're shaking," Reuben whispered.

She wished he hadn't said anything because now she could acutely feel every single muscle tensing. At one time, she had joked with Willow that all this trauma would be worth it if she got a six-pack out of it, but in reality she had put on a few extra pounds. Probably due to the late-night crunching on Craisins and dry Cheerios.

"You know," the fur lady continued loud enough for everyone in the car to hear, "my husband and I are big supporters of Pastor Carl's mission to unwed mothers." Her earrings jingled ostentatiously as she nodded her head up and down. "A great ministry."

Reuben stared at Kennedy in concern. Sometimes his sympathy was harder to bear than her own mess of emotions. He would get to looking at her like she was a dying butterfly about to take its last flutter. How was she supposed to forget about the past and move on when everyone kept reminding her about it?

"I was telling my husband," Fur Lady continued, "those women sure need our help. You know, back in my day, when a gal got pregnant, she would either marry the boy or she'd put the baby up for adoption to be raised by a real family. Nowadays, it seems like all these girls want is a baby or two, no matter if there's a dad in the picture or not.

The state pays more with each kid, you know, and then of course these girls go and demand child support. You get enough babies lined up and make the state and those dads all shell out their cash, and you can make a good living without lifting a finger."

Kennedy bit her lip and glanced around. The man near the exit glared from over the top of his magazine. Just a few more stops. If she could handle complex computations during a lab titration without using a calculator, she could keep her mouth shut for a few more minutes on the T with a rude, loud-mouthed busybody.

"In fact," the woman prattled on, "I was at the store just the other day, and one of those welfare moms came up with her coupons ..."

The T jolted to an unexpected stop, and the woman let out an unbecoming expletive. The lights flickered once and then went off.

"What was that?" she screeched, her voice rising to an even more annoying pitch, somewhat akin to a silver fork scraping against a ceramic plate.

"Must be having some kind of problems with the T," a man answered. Several passengers pulled out their phones and let the light from the screens pierce through the darkness.

Kennedy tried to ignore the fluttering in her heart. Things like this probably happened all the time. Nothing to worry about. Nothing at all. She scooted a little closer to Reuben.

"Maybe it's the wind," someone suggested. "Coulda blown down the electrical lines."

"Welcome to Boston," muttered another.

Beside her, Reuben sat as calm as always. He was probably enjoying the extra time to think about his favorite scenes from *The Nutcracker*. She pressed her hands to her throbbing temples. There was too much work to do. She still wasn't packed for her trip to her aunt's tomorrow, and she had to be up early to meet with Detective Drisklay. She had to get in touch with Adell to see if she needed to retake the exam tomorrow morning or if it would count as an excused absence. She'd be a little disappointed if she didn't have to take it at all. What kind of school would let someone out of a final because of a cough? It wasn't fair to the other students. It wasn't even fair to Kennedy, given the hours she had spent studying.

"How long until we start going again?" asked the woman in the fur coat. "Shouldn't the conductor say something on that system of his?"

"Power's out," a passenger mumbled. "No way for him

to tell us anything."

"So we just stay here?" Her voice rose higher. Kennedy wanted to cover her ears.

"They'll get it up and going soon enough."

"Are you cold?" Reuben took off his parka.

"You really don't need to. I'm all right." Why did she always do that? Why did she always pretend that she was hanging on better than she really was?

He draped his jacket around her shoulders. She stretched her arms into the soft nylon. His warmth still clung to the inside, wrapping her up like a foam insulator around a lab flask. Like a warm hug on a cold, blustery night.

"Any minute now," he said. "We'll be moving again soon."

His coat smelled like the student union. The student union and all of Reuben's favorite foods. Pizza, Doritos, plenty of bacon. The faint scent of smoke.

Smoke?

"What is that?" the fur lady screeched as grayish fog filled the car from the bottom up.

The passengers jumped to their feet in a noisy, confused jumble. Everyone spoke at once. Kennedy held her breath. What was going on?

"Where's it coming from?" someone asked. A few passengers coughed.

"There. I see something over there." Several phones flashed their lights to a corner of the car where smoke piled more densely around the fur lady's feet. She let out a little wail and rushed on her high heels to the far side of the T as the smoke billowed up to the level of their waists.

The smell was stronger, a mix of melting plastic and something else that stung Kennedy's sinuses. Most of the passengers covered their faces with their scarfs or sleeves. Reuben held her arm. How were they supposed to get out? She glanced around, trying to guess what her dad would do in a situation like this. He had safety protocols for any type of crisis — getting kidnapped, getting mugged, getting carjacked. Before she left for Harvard, he even made her role-play what she would do if a professor threatened to lower her grade unless she slept with him. All those ridiculous hypotheticals, all that paranoid crisis training, but he never once thought to tell her what to do if she got stuck on a burning subway car during an electrical outage.

The smoke swirled higher and stung her eyes. She hid her face in the collar of Reuben's parka. Her empty stomach swirled, and voices flew by her, hardly perceived. *The extinguisher ... Pull that pin ... What if it's electric ...*

Aim toward the bottom. Shouting. Chaos. Kennedy tried to conserve her breaths. She had to get out.

The strange, almost sweet smell of the fire extinguisher spray. The sound of a dozen passengers sighing as one, but Kennedy's lungs remained paralyzed in her chest.

No, not again. Not here.

More voices. Relief and fear mingled in their tones. *Got it ... Still smells like smoke ...*

She coughed. That wasn't the extinguisher fluid stinging her lungs.

Still just as bad ... More smoke ... Out of spray.

"Open the doors!"

Banging on windows. A walking stick swinging overhead. The thud of glass refusing to give.

The man who had been reading the magazine jostled the lever of the emergency exit. Fresh air. Everybody surged toward the opening. *Ladies first ... Make room ... Not all at once ...*

Hands reaching out, grabbing her shoulders, propelling her forward. All she could think about was getting out of the car. Out of the tunnel.

Watch your step ... Gonna be all right.

She hopped off the train, and another passenger held out his hand and helped her to a small sidewalk running alongside the tunnel. Bending over, she coughed until her lungs were clear, thankful the choking didn't set off another crying fit. She was safe. She was off the T. Everything was going to be just fine.

CHAPTER 7

It took Kennedy a moment or two to adjust to her new surroundings. She was standing on some kind of platform, narrower than a city sidewalk. She touched the wall to steady herself and immediately snatched back her hand, her spine prickling at the thought of all the germs she had just contracted. She reached instinctively for the Germ X in her backpack, only then remembering she had left her bag on the T. She rubbed her grimy fingers together, her nose and cheeks crinkling in disgust.

She stepped farther down the platform. If she had her phone with her, she could have shined some extra light on the path, but of course she had left that behind in her backpack as well. It would be easier to keep her cell in her pocket like every other college student she knew, but the thought of all that radiation sitting right next to her made her skin feel hot and scorched.

Any minute, she expected Reuben to materialize beside her. What was taking him so long? And why didn't the

MBTA keep some kind of emergency lights down here, anyway? It was so dark. She shut her eyes and inhaled. It was all right. She was in a subway tunnel. They had encountered some technical difficulties, but the T lines were so old, the cars so decrepit, this was probably a regular occurrence. Maybe the MBTA would give them all free passes for a year or something as recompense.

So much smoke. She hadn't known a car could fill that fast.

Kennedy took another few steps away from the train. What if the smoke had come from a bomb? What if it exploded? She thought about the action movies she and her dad liked to watch together, how the hero would leap forward as a fireball blasted behind, outlining him in glorious shades of red and orange. The explosion always gave an extra push but never really injured anybody. Maybe a few scrapes, a small bruise if the directors wanted to be gritty. But Kennedy knew the science behind an explosion in an enclosed space like this. It wouldn't matter if she was five feet away or fifty. She inched down the platform to put more distance between herself and the train. She didn't see any flames. That was a good sign. When would Reuben come out?

Submerged memories forced their way to the surface of

her mind. Handcuffs, the sharp metal digging into her wrist. The ache in her back from spending a whole night chained on the couch. The crawl of her skin in her squalid surroundings. Images of lice and bedbugs and rodents growing to IMAX proportions on her brain's mental projector. She hurried farther away from the train, picking up speed as her boots clanked against the cement.

She was panting now. She heard the sound of her own breathing but couldn't control the rate. Cold. Why couldn't they at least give her a blanket to wrap up in? The feel of a small child shivering next to her, a child far too young to be trapped with her, a child Kennedy could do nothing to help.

She drew in a sharp breath. She was in a subway station, not handcuffed in a cement basement. It was dark because she was in a tunnel, not because her captors had blindfolded her. She was still free. Nobody was keeping her here against her will. She could walk away whenever she wanted. Nobody would point a gun at her or pull a knife to make her stay.

Forgetting what is behind.

The heat of anger mingled with the chill of fear, and her gut sizzled with steam at the spot where they met. Why couldn't she get over these silly anxieties? She could tackle twenty-two credits this semester, find time to take her self-defense class, and even read a few books a month just for fun. Why couldn't she get a grip over her own thoughts instead of letting them trap her into the past whenever they felt like tormenting her?

The old has gone, the new has come. Kennedy quoted one of the verses she had memorized during a recent quiet time. *Take every thought captive* was another good one. That's what she had to do. Seize her thoughts. Seize those horrible, relentless memories. Lock them up where she could control them. Give them nothing but water to sip, deprive them of warmth, feed them only on fear. Fear that she would never be rescued. Fear that her captors would murder her and nobody would find out for weeks. Fear that she would have to stand by and watch an innocent child die at the hands of godless, soulless monsters.

She pressed her fingernails into her palms. No, this wasn't the way to walk in victory. This wasn't the way to find her freedom and deliverance. If God could take the sins of the world and throw them into the sea of forgetfulness, surely Kennedy could do the same thing to a few old memories that still haunted her. If she only knew how. More prayer, maybe. More Bible reading. She had gotten so busy with finals she had let her spiritual disciplines slide. That's why she was suffering now. That's why she felt like the wild rabbit, crouching in plain sight with no hope of shelter or safety, knowing the fox would pounce with its razor teeth but unable to guess when.

Steps on the sidewalk. She felt the vibrations just a yard or two away. "Reuben?" she asked, her voice quiet. So uncertain. "Is that you?"

No answer. Kennedy held her breath. What had her self-defense instructor said? She couldn't let her brain shut down when she was scared. She had to channel that fear and turn it into positive survival energy.

"Is someone there?" She sounded more like a mouse, her words a pitiful squeal.

No, that wasn't who Kennedy was anymore. She didn't have to be afraid. She knew how to protect herself. She even had her pepper spray. Wait, that was still on the T along with everything else. Why hadn't she remembered to take her backpack with her?

"Don't get any closer. Stay where you are." She tried not to sound too forceful. What would people think of her? It was probably just another passenger getting off the train. How had she gotten so far from the main group in the first place?

She hurried down the walkway. The footsteps echoed behind. She glanced over her shoulder. "You need to stop following me." Kennedy spoke assertively like she had practiced in her class. She had been so self-conscious those first few times she had to stare her instructor right in the eye and say ridiculous things like, "Get back five feet," or "No, you're making me uncomfortable, and I want you to leave." But nothing had been as awkward as the simulations when they brought in male volunteers to attack the students. She hoped to never suffer through something that humiliating again, whether in a controlled role-play setting or in real life.

Hot breath tickled her neck. Or was that just her imagination? If she reached out her arm, she would know for sure if someone was there. But what if he grabbed her? What if Vinny had escaped custody? What if he followed her and was just waiting for the chance to get her alone?

She wouldn't be victimized again. She had to get away. She wouldn't let him catch up to her. A footstep on the concrete. Not a fabrication. Not this time. It was real. Real as the scientific method. Real as her parents' love for her. Real as death. In the pitch darkness, she rushed ahead, running her fingers along the grimy wall so she would know which way to go as she sprinted down the walkway. What did contracting a few germs compare to getting murdered?

How close was he now? And why couldn't she have remembered her pepper spray? She strained her ears but only heard the slap of her boots on the walkway, the sound of her own panting, the pounding of her heart valves in her pericardial sac. She didn't want to stop, couldn't slow down, but she had to save her strength. She needed energy to fight back when he caught up. She couldn't hear him, but that didn't mean he wasn't coming.

Any second now.

CHAPTER 8

Kennedy rehearsed every lesson from her self-defense class in fast motion, promised herself never to roll her eyes at her dad for all his unsolicited safety advice. Legs in a crouch, back hip at a slight angle. Hands up, ready to block, ready for a blow. Should she go for a throat strike with the fingers or palm strike to the chin? Her ears pounded as her heart plunged blood and oxygen and adrenaline to every muscle cell in her body.

Kennedy stood as still as the fetal pig corpse she had dissected in high school. She prayed for protection, not in actual words but in that unspoken language of desperation, hopes shot heavenward with the full expectation God could understand and decipher her soul's chaotic pleading. She strained to pick up the slightest noise around her. Nothing. Not even the voices of the people evacuated from the T.

Why had she separated herself from the group? She should have raced back toward Reuben and the others the second she suspected someone was following her. Even if that sped up the inevitable confrontation, she would have been close enough for people to help. For people to hear her scream. Now she was cut off. Stranded. Completely unprotected. No witnesses. How far had she been running? What would happen if they found her body on the tracks tomorrow morning? Fears of radiation and cancer aside, she vowed to never ride the subway again without carrying her phone in her pocket. Her phone and her pepper spray.

Stupid. Stupid what you do when you're so afraid your neural circuits shut down one after another like a domino effect of idiocy. Isn't that what her self-defense instructors had warned her about? Isn't that why they ran her through all those painfully awkward simulations, so she could think straight when her veins flooded with epinephrine and her mind clouded with the rush of fear?

Kennedy took a deep breath. There was nothing to hear, nothing around her but perfect stillness. If she didn't know better, she might have thought herself the only human in a twenty-mile radius. She should go back. The farther she went down the rail, the more she distanced herself from people who might help her. If there really was someone after her in the first place. What if this was just another attack, a trick of her brain that now seemed to think trauma was a normal, everyday part of life, something to fabricate if reality didn't provide enough danger?

Part of her wanted to reach out, touch the phantom that had scared her so badly, figure out exactly what had made her run. Probably not even a person at all. She thought about *Little House in the Big Woods*. As a little girl, she had giggled wildly at the part when Pa was walking home late and saw a bear blocking his path. After a terrifying standoff in which the bear didn't move a muscle, Pa finally charged it with a stick only to find that he had been having a stare-down with an old tree stump. It had been hilarious back then, picturing Pa with his big broad shoulders and his long scruffy beard getting scared by a silly shadow. Kennedy had never thought until now about the way his heart must have thudded underneath his flannel shirt, how his thoughts must have turned homeward to Ma and the girls, wondering if he would ever see their faces or hold them in his arms again.

Kennedy shook her head. How had she let her own silly fears drive her this far down the tracks? It was probably the stress of finals week. Her meeting tomorrow with Detective Drisklay. How long until she could forget about the entire ordeal and get on with a normal life?

It was silly to stay here and shiver in the dark. She had to get back to Reuben. He was probably worried about her by now. What would he say when he found out she had run so far on account of a few unfamiliar sounds? Kennedy smoothed his coat she was still wearing. It was time to go back. He might tease her, and then it would be over. At least she'd be safe. She'd probably been safe all along. Now she just wanted to get back to Reuben, get back to campus. Tomorrow would be another long, busy day. The semester was over, and now she wanted to relax. Get back to her dorm, maybe read a little from her Turgenev book, grab a snack, and then go to sleep. She could take her laundry to Aunt Lilian's and wash it there.

She still couldn't believe what she had done. What would her self-defense instructors say if they saw what a coward she had been? How would they chide her for running away from the group of potential witnesses instead of toward them? That silly class probably made her even more paranoid than she needed to be, all those scenarios she had to act out, all that talk about what horrible situations she might find herself in one day. Just like Pa and the bear in the woods. Only it had been a tree stump.

She stepped slowly at first, thinking up the least embarrassing way to tell Reuben why she had freaked out and run a quarter mile or more in an unlit underground tunnel.

She let out her breath, the sound of her sigh even louder than normal in the enclosed space. She thought about the chapter in *Les Miserables*, the fifty pages or more Victor Hugo devoted to verbose descriptions of the underground sewer system in Paris. How would Hugo paint the tunnels beneath the streets of Boston if he were alive today?

Yes, she would think about *Les Miserables*. Even before she read the book, her mom took her to see the Broadway show when they still lived in New York. She had loved the music as a child and let the lyrics run through her mind. Another few minutes and she'd be back with Reuben. Then they could go back to …

Slam. The thud of a shoe pounding the pavement. So there was someone after all. He was behind her now. How had he circled around on the other side? It didn't matter. She was running, pushing forward, lunging ahead.

Noise. She needed to make noise. There wasn't time to recall those forceful sayings she had practiced in self-defense. So she screamed. At least she tried to. It came out more like a squeal. It didn't sound particularly bold or courageous, and it wasn't even loud. Not as loud as his boots smashing into the cement. Any minute now, she would get tackled from behind, but she didn't have time to plan and visualize how she would fight him off. Getting away and making as much ruckus as she could — that was the only plan.

She surged forward, her heart close to bursting from exertion. Her only other feeling was the pain in her shins, the sting in her lungs. He was right behind her. She pictured him reaching out his hand, knew he was about to jerk her to a dead stop, braced herself so the whiplash wouldn't be so bad. She arched her back, as if gaining another centimeter or two of distance could delay the inevitable.

Please, Lord, get me out of this.

"Watch out!"

By the time she realized the voice was in front of her, she didn't have a chance to slow herself down. She slammed into him, and her breath rushed out of her chest. They both stumbled. He grabbed her by the shoulders to keep them both from falling, and all those simple moves she had practiced in self-defense deserted her. There was no reflex reaction, no autonomic response. Instead, she froze, and he gripped her by both shoulders. Almost as an afterthought, she tried to thrash her body to throw him off, and for a minute, she was afraid they'd both topple over the edge onto the rails below.

"Calm down." He wrapped his arms tight around her,

and her brain stopped trying to recall how to get out of a bear hug and instead focused on his voice. "It's me."

"Reuben?" Saying his name unleashed a torrent of tears, and he held her, whispering comforting words that made her feel even more wretched.

Kennedy shook her head. "Someone was coming."

Reuben took out his cellphone and let its glow fall on the tracks and walkway around them. "I don't see anybody."

"I was being chased. He was right ..." Kennedy stopped. *Pa and the bear.* If she could have turned into a corrosive acid, burned a hole into the cement, and disappeared from sight, she would have.

"I'm sorry." She sniffed, afraid to get some of the snot from her runny nose on Reuben's coat.

"Another episode?" Reuben offered quietly.

She turned her face away. God was merciful to have turned off the lights. Now she wouldn't have to look Reuben in the eye. Not yet, anyway. She would have been willing to stay there in the darkness forever, but once she started breathing a little calmer he said, "We're only a few hundred yards from the Boylston station. You think you're ready to walk?"

"I'm sorry," Kennedy repeated. This was supposed to

be a fun night. Why couldn't life be more like the chem lab? If you didn't get it right the first time, you could just dump everything down the drain and start over fresh. "I'm such an idiot."

"No, you're not." The good-natured teasing never came. The playful jabs, nothing. "You've been really stressed out. This kind of thing doesn't mix well with stress. You know?"

No, Kennedy didn't know. Reuben could talk about *this kind of thing*, but what was it really? She recalled the large, scrawling letters the doctor wrote on the notepad. *Post-traumatic stress disorder.* But he was wrong. He had to be.

"You ready?" Reuben asked and shined the light from his cell on the walkway in front of them.

Kennedy swallowed through the tightness in her throat. "Yeah. I'm ready."

When they passed the train car, the smoke was gone. The conductor and a firefighter pointed their flashlights at the tracks. Most of the passengers had gone. Kennedy was thankful she didn't have to meet anyone's eye.

"I got your backpack," Reuben told her, patting the straps on his shoulders. This was the second time he had retrieved her bag for her when she had one of her ... *episodes*, or whatever they were. Any other night, she might have made a joke about being careful so this sort of thing didn't become a habit, but her humor as well as her energy were stuck back there in the subway tunnel, pounded into the ground where her feet had smashed the pavement. Her heart rate was steadier now, but her stomach churned with the bitter aftertaste of humiliation.

"What's that light ahead?" she asked.

"I think that's the Boylston station."

Kennedy squinted. "I thought the power was out." She would have preferred the darkness, at least for a little while longer.

Reuben slowed down. "I heard the conductor and the firemen talking. It sounds like the problem was localized. Something on the subway grid." He adjusted the straps of Kennedy's backpack. "Do you still want that pizza?"

"No, thanks." There was only one thing Kennedy wanted to do — get home and forget this night ever happened. Maybe Reuben was right. Maybe she should talk to somebody about her episodes. She hated the idea of rehashing her abduction all over again, but could it be worse than being a slave to these fears? How many more tests would she miss? What would happen if she fell victim to an attack while working with dangerous chemicals in the lab?

When they stepped into the lights of Boylston station,

Kennedy wished she could wrap her scarf around her entire face, not just her neck. She avoided Reuben's eyes and everyone else's. Could these strangers tell just by looking at her that she was crazy? Maybe even delusional?

What was wrong with her? Was it just stress from finals, maybe? Lack of sleep? Or was she truly losing her mind? No, crazy people never worried about going crazy, did they? It was only sane people who questioned their sanity, right?

Home. Well, at least the closest thing she had to a home in the States. Willow would be at Cape Cod for the next few days before she flew back to Alaska. Kennedy wouldn't have to answer any questions, engage with anybody. Home. She glanced at the map of the T. Five stops and one transfer would get her back to her dorm in half an hour or so. Maybe less if there were no more delays. Could she do it? Could she force herself to step onto another subway?

Just a malfunction, she told herself, but her lungs still stung with the memory of smoke, and her pulse quickened at the sound of an oncoming train. What if she had lost her balance running away from phantoms in the dark? What if she had landed on the tracks and knocked herself out and nobody found her before …?

Reuben slipped his hand into his pocket, flipped casually through his wallet. "How would you feel about taking a taxi?"

Kennedy didn't know how shallow her breaths had grown until her lungs let out one prolonged, choppy sigh. "That sounds like a really good idea."

CHAPTER 9

"You don't need to keep telling me you're sorry." Reuben leaned against the doorway of Kennedy's dorm room. "Did you know you apologized five times in the taxi?"

Kennedy still wished Reuben had let her pay the fare. She was thrilled to be as far away from the subway system as possible, but it wasn't as if Reuben had a whole lot of discretionary income. She didn't, either, but she would have felt less guilty about plunking fifteen bucks on a taxi ride back to campus if it had been her money, not his.

"So, you're really all right?" Reuben stalled at the door. On any other night, Kennedy might have thought it was sweet. Right now, she only wanted to get to bed. All the energy she had exhausted getting ready for finals had finally caught up to her. She was drained, sucked dry like a pile of old Craisins left out on her desk. She needed sleep.

"Maybe we can hang out again when I get back from Maryland," she suggested. "Rain check?"

"Rain what?" Reuben was even worse at American idioms than she was.

"Rain check. Since tonight didn't work for pizza, we can do it when I get back from Maryland. Deal?"

Reuben flashed her a thumbs up. "It's a deal."

"I promise I won't chicken out on you next time."

"Chicken?"

"Never mind."

Sleep. She wanted to sleep. Her bed beckoned to her with its own irresistible gravity.

He stepped into her room and gave her an awkward half-hug. "Merry Christmas."

"You, too." Heaviness sank in her gut, disappointment over their failed night out mingling with her own embarrassment. She plopped onto the bed. Why did she always do this to herself? She had let her own anxiety and nerves ruin her evening out with Reuben, and now she didn't even have the strength to pack her bags for tomorrow. The morning would come all too soon.

She set her alarm for seven. That would give her time to start her laundry and see if Adell wanted her to come in for her final. And then she had to be at the detective's by ten. Why hadn't she asked him if they could get together after Christmas vacation? With Vinny in custody, what was the rush?

Her head hit the pillow, and she wondered how many cavities she'd end up with if she went a night without brushing her teeth. She'd have to get up soon, but she'd take a minute or two to rest her eyes first. She deserved at least that small indulgence, didn't she?

The whole dorm was as still and lifeless as a dish full of fruit flies etherized into temporary comas. Everyone had already rushed home to their moms and dads, to their decorated houses and colorful Christmas trees. The silence was like pin pricks in Kennedy's ears, and she missed the ticking of the grandfather clock in her parents' house back in Yanji.

Just a few minutes' rest. Then she'd get up and do something productive. She couldn't sleep the whole night away …

All she could focus on was the exhaustion in her limbs and the gnawing emptiness in her gut. They hadn't fed her in almost a day. Water. Just a little sip of water.

Tinkering. Stockpiles of weapons. Men fiddling by the workbench. Arguing in hushed tones.

Blood. A whole river of it. How could someone so little lose that much?

Lights. Flashing. Strobing. Ringing sirens. Never stopping.

Breathe. She couldn't breathe.

Kennedy opened her mouth and inhaled noisily. Oxygen flooded her brain, jolting her into consciousness. She sat up in bed, gasping. Her body was cold and clammy with sweat. She hadn't even taken her black boots off.

The ringing continued. Her phone. She glanced at the clock. Past eleven. Who would be calling now?

She flipped on her desk lamp, which cast dim shadows on Willow's side of the room. She checked the caller ID.

"Dad?" Her voice was croaky from sleepiness. She hoped he couldn't tell how confused she felt.

"Honey, where are you?" His voice was even more tense than normal.

"I'm in my dorm."

"Did you lock yourself in?"

Kennedy rubbed her eyes. Did her dad really think a safety drill at this time of the night would help anything?

"Did you lock yourself in?" he demanded again.

Kennedy let her eyes drift slowly to her door. She couldn't even remember what time it was when she lay down. "Mmm-hmmm," she lied, staring at the unbolted lock.

Her dad let out his breath in a sigh that did nothing to relieve the strain from his voice. "I was just on Channel 2's webpage. Have you heard about Vinny?"

Kennedy contemplated whether it was worth getting off her soft mattress to lock herself in. She probably should, she decided without moving. "Yeah. They caught him just yesterday." Or was it two days ago? She couldn't figure it out. Was it tomorrow yet, or still today?

"Not that. They say he's been working with a partner. A man who's wanted for questioning. Sounds like he was part of the plot last fall."

This was news to Kennedy, but she still didn't understand why it couldn't have waited for morning. "I'll ask Detective Drisklay about it tomorrow." Was that the only reason her dad had called?

"Is your computer up?" he asked.

"No, I've been asleep for the past couple hours." Had it really been that long? She had only meant to take a little catnap.

"Well, I'm emailing you the news page. It's got a

picture of the man. I want you to take a good look at it. If he was involved with everything that happened, he's not going to want you talking to the police, or anyone else for that matter."

"Yeah, I'll take a look." She stood up. Her back was as tight as a spring scale.

"I'm sending it now. Check your email as soon as we hang up."

"I will." She shoved some dirty clothes into her laundry bag. Her back and leg muscles ached. Had she really been running that far in the subway tunnel?

"All right, sweetheart. How were your exams?" he added, almost like an afterthought.

"They went fine." Kennedy was ready to forget about them.

Her dad paused for just a moment and then added, "Well, have a safe trip to your aunt's tomorrow. Remember, call ..."

"I'll call you as soon as the plane lands," Kennedy interrupted. "Talk to you later."

"I love you, sweetie."

"Love you, too."

Kennedy put the phone on her desk. Stupid laundry. Stupid dreams. Stupid evening. For a minute, she wondered if Reuben was awake. Well, she wouldn't bother him now. She needed time to let her bruised pride heal over. She'd get back to campus in a few weeks in time to start a new semester. She and Reuben would take general chemistry, chem lab, and calculus together again, and things would go just like this term. Joking in the cafeteria. Late nights in the library. Frantic texts the day before a lab was due. It almost would have made things easier if he had laughed at her in the taxi. Now, she was mortified not only by her own behavior but by his undeserved compassion.

Kennedy fumbled through her desk looking for spare change for the laundromat. Her phone buzzed with an incoming text.

Emailed you the link. Did you get it?

She had already forgotten about the news from Channel 2. When would her life stop being ruled by current events her dad read from halfway around the world?

Reading it right now, she typed back, but her phone powered off before she could send it.

Stupid battery.

She thought about going back to bed. Her dad had only said there was another potential suspect. If the police thought she was in danger, they would have called to let her know. Just like her dad to ruin a perfect nap with his paranoia.

Still, if she didn't give him some sort of response, she'd never hear the end of it tomorrow. She clicked on her computer and waited for her inbox to open. There was a note from Adell telling her she could take the test when she got back to campus in January, and there was another note from her Russian lit professor. She had gotten an A on her paper on Raskonikov and the Christological symbols in the epilogue of *Crime and Punishment*. "If you were a grad student, I'd encourage you to get your ideas published." It was a somewhat indirect compliment, but Kennedy would take it anyway.

After shooting back quick replies to both professors, she clicked on the email from her dad. No notes attached, no *Merry Christmas, sweetheart*, just the web address for a Channel 2 webpage. She opened it up, hoping it wouldn't take too long to load. She needed to get her clothes washed.

Additional Partner Identified in Boston Kidnapping Case. At least when she got to Maryland, nobody there would remember the incident. Even if they did, they would consider it old news.

She skimmed the text, her eyes darting down the screen so she could tell her dad she read the whole thing. Four paragraphs down, she froze. The computer was still loading the bottom half of his face, but she recognized his eyes immediately.

Cold. Icy green like frosted grass before it's covered by snow and trampled by sleds.

The picture kept loading. High cheeks. Angular nose.

Tight jaw. Lips drawn in a narrow line.

The man from the subway.

A noise in the hall. Kennedy whipped her head up from her computer screen in time to see her doorknob turn.

CHAPTER 10

She imagined screaming but was too petrified to make an actual sound. She pictured herself running behind the door so that when it swung open she would be partially concealed behind it. But her feet fastened to the ground like a slide on a microscope stage, held in place by unyielding metal clips. Her scream stuck between her throat and her mouth, closing off her trachea so she couldn't breathe.

She watched the door swing toward her, clutched her phone as if it could ward off an attack. Blood drained from her head to her limbs, which still refused to move.

"What are you standing in the middle of the room for?"

At the sight of her roommate, Kennedy's breath whooshed out of her lungs like wind through the subway tunnel. The paralyzing power of fear melted, and embarrassment heated her face. She steadied herself against her desk and clicked off her monitor. "Oh, you startled me, that's all. I was just talking with my dad."

Willow raised an eyebrow and glided in, leaving the

door partially open behind her. *Lock us in here*, Kennedy wanted to scream. She forced a smile. How many times would she humiliate herself before the night was over? "What are you doing? I thought you were going right from Cape Cod to the airport."

Willow tossed her long raven waves over her shoulder. Of all the hair colors Willow had gone through this semester, Kennedy liked black the best. It reminded her of those smooth onyx gems her grandmother used to buy for her at the little knick-knack shop in upstate New York. Kennedy had loved the soft feel of the stones, which could stay several degrees cooler than the ambient temperature.

Willow tossed her duffel bag onto her bed. "The partying was lame."

Kennedy tried to hide her surprise. Willow hadn't talked about anything besides her trip to the Cape during all of finals week. She and about a dozen of her theater friends had rented a little cottage, and Willow had rattled off their inventory of entertainment plans — both legal and illegal — nearly every night like a bedtime prayer.

"Besides," Willow continued, "I got a text from this guy I met at the bakery. He thought it might be fun to get together, so I left early." She plopped onto her mattress and studied her fingernails which were painted with the swirling colors of the aurora borealis. "Anyway, what'd you do tonight? Eat Cheerios and stick your nose in a book?"

Kennedy had to chuckle at how well Willow knew her. "Actually, I was out with Reuben. We saw *The Nutcracker.*"

"It's about time you two finally started to date."

Kennedy fidgeted with some old papers on her desk. Maybe she should clean up a little before she left for Maryland. "It wasn't a date." Kennedy's back tingled at the spot where she knew Willow was staring.

Willow let out a dramatic sigh. "You two are so cute together. Just going slow like you both have all the time in the world. It's adorable."

Kennedy's brain was too groggy to defend herself or Reuben.

"Anyway," Willow prattled on, smacking gum while she talked, "you know I totally respect your morals and everything. Because if I didn't, I would have figured he was gay or something and that's why you hadn't hooked up yet."

Kennedy's whole stomach scrunched as if someone was trying to twist excess water out of it. She hoped her expression was more neutral.

"Boy, you look tired," Willow exclaimed and kicked off her shoes. "Are you ok? Wait." She stood back up. "He didn't hurt your or anything, did he?"

Kennedy was itchy beneath her sweater. Itchy and sweaty. "No, nothing like that."

"Good. Because, honestly, from the looks of it, you're either doped up or something freaked you out. So what is it?"

Kennedy inhaled choppily. Maybe she needed acting lessons from Willow. "Nothing. I'm fine."

Willow raised her eyebrows, which were about as thin as two blades of grass.

"It's just my dad," Kennedy explained. "I guess he read in the news that there's now another suspect at large."

Willow frowned. "He give you one of his famous freak-out safety speeches? Well that explains the shell-shock." She chuckled. "For a minute, I was worried it was serious."

Something buzzed, and Kennedy flinched at the noise.

"Geez, woman. You're as jumpy as a poodle in heat." Willow reached into her pocket and smirked at the screen. "It's just a text from the guy I met. He's an actor. Hey, let me get on your computer. I want to see if he's got an IMBD page." She turned on the monitor and froze when the Channel 2 page leapt onto the screen. Her eyes widened, and she brought her blanched face closer to Kennedy's computer screen. "Where'd you get this picture?"

Unease splashed at the bottom of Kennedy's gut and sent waves of fear rippling outward. "That's the guy I told you about. The one they think helped mastermind things last fall." Even now Kennedy couldn't bring herself to use words like *kidnapping*. "I forget his name. Something kinda ethnic. Guido? Giulio?"

"Gino." Willow's voice, usually dripping with melodrama, was terse. Expressionless.

Kennedy's legs felt like they were supporting one of Boston's looming concrete overpasses. "What are you talking about?"

Willow pointed at the computer screen, but Kennedy didn't even want to look. What venom dripped from that photograph? What new threats would she discover in that pixelated image?

Willow slammed her fist on Kennedy's desk. "No, no, no, no, no." She pinched her forehead between her thumb and forefinger. "The jerk!" If Kennedy had been critiquing one of her roommate's plays, she would say Willow was overdoing it. Willow held out her hand in the universal sign for *Don't freak out on me.* "That guy in the photo, that's the one I met at the bakery. The one I was supposed to ..."

Willow scrunched up a large handful of her jet-black hair. "We've been texting all night, making plans for tomorrow. I gave him our dorm number and everything."

CHAPTER 11

Kennedy's diastolic blood pressure must have dropped at least twenty points. She didn't yell. Raising her voice might attract whatever fiend her roommate had invited. *Seriously? Seriously!* Willow was always hooking up with strangers, but a random man at least in his thirties she met at a bakery?

"When's he coming over?" Kennedy's voice quivered, but she didn't care. Disgust and fear warred against each other in her stomach. It was a miracle she didn't have a dozen ulcers after a semester like this.

"We weren't going to meet until tomorrow," Willow answered. "You know I don't do that kind of stuff until you're out."

Kennedy shut her eyes. *Think.* She had to think. Come up with a plan. Which was harder than it sounded after functioning on a few hours of sleep each night. Why did her parents have to live so far away?

Willow picked up her duffel. "Come on. Are you

already packed for tomorrow?" She grabbed Kennedy's backpack and shoved it at her.

"What are you doing?"

"We're not staying here," Willow answered. "We'll spend the night with Toby."

"The RA?"

Willow put her shoes back on, but Kennedy still hadn't moved.

"Let's go." Willow stopped tugging on her laces. "Look, Toby and I will behave ourselves. I promise. Nothing funny. Now hurry up before Gino decides to pay a surprise visit."

Kennedy stared around the room, uncertain what to take. She still had that mass of laundry, and her clean clothes were strewn sloppily in her drawers. Her mind was swarming, like a chemical reaction that clogs up if you introduce too many reagents at once. She stared at her dead cellphone, her lifeline to her parents. To emergency responders.

Willow was right. They should both go somewhere else. But would they be any safer down the hall? The men who abducted her last October were chillingly high-tech. They had bugged her phone, hacked her computer. What difference would it make if she were in her own dorm or five rooms down when Gino came after her?

But what other choices did she have? She couldn't ask Reuben to put her up for the night. It would be ridiculously awkward, for one thing. For another, she didn't have his phone number memorized and couldn't call him until her phone charged. Where was the plug?

"You're stalling." Willow's hand was on the doorknob, her penciled eyebrows slanted down.

"I just can't figure out what would be best." With all the crisis training her dad put her through, you'd think she'd be more prepared to make these sorts of snap decisions. Maybe he was right. Maybe she just wasn't ready to be out on her own yet. "Do you think we should call the police?"

"Of course. But not from here." Willow's features softened, her eyebrows resumed their regular position, and she sighed. "I know this is all my fault. And I'm really sorry. I thought that he … well, he wasn't what I expected. Now I just want to make things right and make sure you're safe, ok? If you're not comfortable at Toby's, then let's find somewhere else to go. Do you have any other ideas?"

Kennedy's stomach rumbled once. Why couldn't this have been a normal night? She should be asleep right now.

Willow's hand rested on the doorknob. Waiting.

Waiting for Kennedy to make up her mind. Only she didn't know how. Kennedy half-expected Willow to come up with a sarcastic jab, but her roommate just stood there. Watching. Waiting.

Kennedy's mind churned like a centrifuge in slow motion. Reuben's wasn't an option. She didn't really have any other friends on campus. There were students she smiled at, a few in her calculus study group she might eat lunch with if they happened to be in the student union at the same time, but nobody else she could call a friend. In fact, she was closer to Pastor Carl and his wife than to anyone else on campus.

That was it.

"What about my pastor's house?"

It wasn't the ideal scenario. Carl's phone number was stuck in her phone as well, and it would be almost midnight by the time they got there. Well, how many times had he and Sandy told her to let them know if there was ever anything she needed? This was definitely something she needed.

"Do you think you could drive me over there?" Kennedy didn't have the route memorized, but she could point Willow in the right direction and let her phone charge up on the way.

Willow frowned, and Kennedy wondered if she'd throw another one of her fits about the evils of organized religion. "I'm thrilled you have somewhere off campus to go," she started, "but I parked all the way in J lot. So that would mean you and me walking at least ten minutes in the dark in a windstorm that's so loud nobody could hear you scream more than ten feet away, and most of the student body and half the security staff have already gone on break."

The temptation was strong to plop down in bed and worry about everything in the morning. She could talk to the detective, head out of state for a few weeks. No, that wasn't going to cut it. Call the police, maybe? See if they could get her some protection? She hated running to them like a damsel in distress, unable to take care of herself, but if she explained that she had actually seen that man on the subway — a subway that ran out of power and filled with smoke ...

Kennedy's head spun, threatening to knock her off balance. The smoke in the T, the invisible phantom in the tunnel, the chase ... So it had been Gino that whole time. The power outage, everything. That hand she was sure was about to reach out and grab her. Only he didn't. Why? What had stopped him? What had saved her?

No, she couldn't think about those things. *God, why have you left me here to deal with all this myself? You tell me to be brave, and then you throw convicts at me ...*

Willow's voice was as soft as her gently waving midnight hair. "I know it's not easy, but I think we need to go. Let's at least head to Toby's. We'll call the police from there, ok?" she coaxed, as if Kennedy were a toddler afraid of getting wet in the kiddie pool.

Kennedy took a deep breath. The plan made sense. She picked up her phone charger and her coat.

Footsteps pounded up the hall. Footsteps coming closer, headed straight to their room. Kennedy froze, staring at the door Willow had left a crack open.

"Kennedy!"

The door burst open.

CHAPTER 12

Kennedy would never believe any of those suspense novels that had the heroines screaming in every chapter. Her breath caught in her throat, every muscle in her body seized up at once, and she stood paralyzed, staring at the form in the doorway.

When she saw Pastor Carl, she wasn't sure if she wanted to throw herself into his arms for a bear hug or collapse on the ground like a lump of gelatinous mold.

"You know him?" Willow asked. She had snatched the hardcover Bible off Kennedy's shelf and held it high above her head.

"It's ok. This is Pastor Carl." She laughed nervously, picturing Willow swinging the huge book in an attempt to ward off an attack. Silly as it looked, it was more than Kennedy had thought to do. "What are you doing here?"

Carl was winded. He put his hands on his knees and bent forward at the waist. "Your dad called me. Explained about that Gino guy, said he was implicated somehow with everything. He asked me to check up on you. I called at least a dozen times and couldn't get through, so I drove over here." He glanced at Willow, who was now holding the Bible at waist level. "You can put that down, Miss. I know a thing or two about defending myself from Bible thumpers."

For the first time in Kennedy's memory, Willow looked sheepish, and she replaced the Bible on its shelf.

"And as for you, young lady." Pastor Carl clasped Kennedy on the shoulder. "You're coming home with us. We'll drive you to Logan tomorrow in time for you to fly to your aunt's."

Kennedy wasn't about to argue. She glanced at Willow, who seemed eager for the chance to excuse herself. "Don't you think you should come, too?" she asked.

Willow shook her head. "Nah. I still might head over to Toby's. You know, just in case."

"You should still call the police." Kennedy studied Willow's eyes. Was she going to take care of herself? "Or do you want me to do it?"

Willow pouted. "No, I will. I'm the one who made a mess of it."

"What are you getting the police involved for?" Carl looked from one girl to the other. "What's been going on?"

"It was me." Willow's voice was completely deflated.

"I met this guy, and I thought he was ..."

"Willow might have accidentally given our dorm room information out, that's all," Kennedy jumped in.

Carl frowned. "You need to come with us too, then. I'm not about to leave you alone by yourself ..."

Willow picked up her duffel. "I'm all right. I was just leaving anyway." She swung the bag over her shoulder.

Just the thought that Willow had talked with anybody involved in the events of last fall curdled the blood beneath Kennedy's skin. "Be safe," she whispered and did her best to offer a reassuring smile.

"Hey, I'll be just fine." Willow pulled her hair behind her ears. "It's not me they want, remember?"

"That's right." Carl prodded both girls into the hall and shut the door behind them. "That's why Kennedy's coming with me, and you're welcome to as well," he added to Willow.

She flashed one of her stage smiles to reveal dazzling white teeth. "Don't worry about me." She lowered her gaze and stared at Kennedy. "You be careful now, all right?"

"I will." Kennedy wondered why it felt like they were saying good-bye. Break was only a few short weeks. "You, too," she whispered and followed Carl down the stairs.

CHAPTER 13

Kennedy couldn't remember the last time she had seen wind like this. It howled around her face, wrapped around her legs, and threatened to suck her breath away.

"I parked just around here." Carl had to shout to be heard.

Kennedy clutched her leather coat across her, wishing for the warm softness of Reuben's parka again. She followed Carl around the corner and saw his maroon Honda.

He fidgeted with the keys until the doors unlocked. "Gonna have to take this baby in soon to have someone look at the wiring. Every time I signal left, the wipers go on."

Kennedy didn't care what they were driving as long as it got them out of the cold and off campus. How could Willow have been so naïve? Giving their dorm number to a total stranger ...

She had to stop thinking like that. It wasn't Willow's fault. Ok, so maybe it was, but she hadn't acted in malice.

Willow was like an untrained puppy. You couldn't really get mad at her, and even if you did, it wouldn't last for long.

Carl strapped the buckle across his chest and pulled it. "Darn thing never gets tight enough." He tugged a few more times and then seemed content. "You ready?"

She nodded.

"Let's go."

There was hardly any traffic. Kennedy had never been on the roads at this time and wondered if they'd have to worry about drunk drivers. At least it was still a weeknight.

Carl turned down the volume to his talk radio station. "So, you've had an exciting evening, by the sound of it."

Kennedy stared at the picture of Carl's grandkids taped to the dashboard.

"You wanna talk about it?" He gave her a quick glance.

No, she didn't want to talk about it, but she knew she would anyway. That was just the way Carl was. He wouldn't make a single demand, probably wouldn't say more than a dozen words, and Kennedy would end up baring her entire soul before they reached his home in Medford.

Carl drummed a little beat on the top of the steering wheel. Kennedy knew he had lived through his share of both trials and excitement. He played pro football for a few years before settling down as a pastor. He started St. Margaret's only five or six years ago, and it was already one of the largest churches in the Cambridge area. New Englanders were by nature fairly tolerant, but she knew he and his wife had experienced a decent amount of flak in the past for their interracial marriage. Maybe that's why he was so easy to talk to. In all their conversations this semester, he had never once made her feel judged. She shut her eyes for a minute, wishing the night would end.

"I hate these silly rotaries." Carl leaned forward and squinted his eyes as he curved onto one of the Boston area's many circular intersections. "Why can't they just put in a traffic light like normal cities?"

Kennedy was surprised at how few Christmas decorations were out, nothing at all like when she was growing up in New York. The one or two businesses that sported lights were about as polished and appealing as a Charlie Brown Christmas tree.

"So you finished your classes finally? How'd they all go?"

Kennedy sighed. She knew Carl would find a way to get her talking, so she may as well stop resisting and get it over with. "I ended up getting an extension for my chemistry final." She told him about her episode during the test. "I felt pretty stupid when I heard they caught Vinny. I mean, I should have been ecstatic with news like that, but really I was just embarrassed."

Carl didn't respond as he whizzed right over a speed bump. The car jostled and made a loud scraping sound that made Kennedy wince.

"So I had to make an appointment at the clinic to get a medical excuse, and the guy I talked to thinks I should have some counseling when I go back for spring semester."

Carl looked over at Kennedy and rushed through a yellow light. "Really? What kind of counseling?" There was a strain in his voice that made Kennedy even more uneasy.

"Something to do with PTSD. You know, probably thinks I'm still not over the whole thing last fall."

"And are you?"

"Traumatized?" She had to fight off her indignation. "No. It could have been a lot worse."

"No, I mean are you over it?"

Kennedy was shaking now. She hoped Carl didn't notice and hugged her arms across her chest. "I mean … I don't know. I'm trying to move on. That's all."

Her throat constricted.

"I've been praying." Her voice was defensive, but she

didn't care. "And reading my Bible. A lot. And I know that if I keep that up, I'm going to be fine. I don't need to sit on a couch and talk with some shrink about what happened."

She sniffed. *Please don't cry*, she begged herself. That was all she'd need to convince Carl she was as big of a basket case as everyone else thought. Tears spilled out from the corners of her eyes, but she looked out her window and refused to acknowledge them.

Carl was silent. The radio talk show host was drawling on about something or other in the Middle East, and then the next minute he moved on to the American public school system. Didn't Carl realize there were at least a dozen stations playing Christmas music this time of year? Kennedy remembered teaching carols to the North Korean refugees who lived with her family in China. On Christmas Eve, they had all sung a Korean version of *Silent Night* a capella in the den, and the sound had given Kennedy chills.

A small black car revved its engine as it sped past them, swerving in its lane, and Carl muttered something about crazy Boston drivers. The radio host was complaining about a new tax proposal when Carl finally spoke up, his voice soft and subdued. "The Bible never says you have to forget something to heal from it."

Kennedy wiped her nose on her sleeve.

"God promises healing, but sometimes that can take years." Carl handed Kennedy a Kleenex. "Sometimes, it doesn't come until the afterlife," he added, almost to himself.

"I just wish that …"

Kennedy stopped herself. Wish what? That she had never gotten abducted? That her dad didn't constantly freak her out with his safety paranoia? That her roommate hadn't given Kennedy's room number to the one person connected to her kidnapping who remained at large?

"I just wish I could go home." A tear splashed onto her seatbelt buckle.

Carl slowed down and passed her another tissue. "You've had a rough semester. It would have been hard for you even without getting kidnapped."

Kennedy wished people would stop using that word. She didn't need to be reminded of what happened to her last fall. Her nightmares did a good enough job of that.

Carl slowly curved the Honda up an overpass ramp. "You shouldn't be hard on yourself. Just because you're a Christian doesn't mean you …"

The black car in front of them slammed to a stop. There was a terrifying crunch accompanied by a jolt. Kennedy sucked in her breath as Carl's forehead bashed into the steering wheel.

CHAPTER 14

"Are you all right? Is anything broken?"

Kennedy had never heard Carl sound frightened before. They were at a dead stop in the middle of the overpass, but he shot his hand out across her chest, as if he wanted to shield her from the impact several seconds too late. The wipers turned on automatically and screeched loudly against the dry windshield.

"I'm all right." She was a little sore on her shoulder where the seatbelt had seized up, but she didn't think she was injured.

There was a small cut on Carl's forehead, but he opened the door and stepped outside. "I'm gonna see if the other driver's all right. What in the world ..." He slammed the door in the middle of his sentence and walked up to the car ahead, smoothing down the front of his coat.

Kennedy opened her door and hopped out, too. If the driver was hurt, Carl might need an extra set of hands. She patted herself down and checked Carl's fender, which was obviously dented, but at least it hadn't buckled all the way in. Good thing Carl hadn't been driving any faster.

The wind rushed across the top of the overpass, and Kennedy took a few steps away from the edge so she wouldn't lose her balance. She was about to join Carl when the door to the black car ahead opened, and a muscular, slightly balding man jumped out.

Gino.

Her body whipped around and started running before her mind had fully processed the danger. She wasn't about to wait and see if Carl's Honda started up after slamming into Gino's car. She sprinted right past it and hurried down the ramp. There were no sidewalks here, but it didn't matter. She had to get as far away from him as possible.

And then she'd need to find someplace to hide.

Cold, wind, and panic were foreign to her now. Her lungs ached, but she didn't dare slow down or look back. She thought she heard Carl calling behind her, but she couldn't be sure. He was probably worried, probably would attribute her actions to another attack. It didn't matter anymore what he thought. If only this were another episode. She would face shame and humiliation every day of her college career to learn this was another phantom her mind had conjured up.

Maybe the other times were just ghosts from her trauma, but this was different. Her mind was surprisingly clear. There was no coughing, no choking, no sobbing like in the science hall. No, this wasn't some psychological hiccup.

This was real.

She had never driven in Cambridge before. She didn't even have a license. She hadn't been paying attention when Carl was driving and had no idea what street she'd be on once she got down off the overpass ramp. It didn't matter. As long as she got to safety, she didn't care where she was.

The street was mostly bare, no houses, only a few storefront businesses that were all closed for the night. Traffic was slow, but there were headlights ahead. Should she flag someone down? What if it was one of Gino's men? What if they had been following for backup, and now they were coming straight toward her?

Tires screeched and squealed on the overpass above. The wind moaned and whipped past her cheeks. She had to stay alert. She could run underneath the overpass, but that would be an obvious hiding place. The sidewalk was lined with streetlights. Why couldn't the city conserve energy at night like they did near her grandma's house in upstate New York?

Her options were limited, but the worst plan of all was to stay put. She had to keep moving. She thought she heard a crash behind her but couldn't slow down to look. *Just move. Just move.*

Her hair had fallen out of its clip and was smacking her face. She would never buy another pair of winter boots again — no matter how cute or stylish — without checking first to see how well she could run in them. There was a side street just ahead. If she could get to it ...

She strained every muscle. Forced her lungs to push through the pain. *Please, God. Just give me a little more strength.*

Her feet pounded the pavement, shooting fire up her shins as she rounded the corner onto a little residential road. This was perfect. Backyards. Fences. Even a doghouse a few homes down. Any shelter would do if it hid her from Gino.

She slowed her pace. The rest of her body was hot and sweaty from running so hard, but her face was raw with cold. Her leg muscles and lower back ached. How many times had she run in the past twenty-four hours?

Warm shame melted the icy cold on her cheeks. What if ...?

No, this wasn't like the other times. That really had

been Gino getting out of that car. She had seen him once on the subway. She had seen his picture again online. She couldn't have made a mistake like that.

Could she?

And what about Willow? Willow said she recognized him, so it wasn't all in Kennedy's mind. He really was after her, right? Or what if her own paranoia had rubbed off on Willow, as well? Had her dad been giving Kennedy so many safety speeches that her roommate got infected, too?

What would she say to Carl?

Carl.

Where was he? She had just left him. She had just run right past ...

The sound of gunfire. She had never heard it before in real life, only in Willow's silly video games and the movies she watched with her dad, but there was no mistaking it. Were they shooting at Carl? Her feet took off beneath her, thrusting her forward. If she could just make it to that dog house ...

The sound of tires squealing. A car taking the corner way too fast. She wasn't going to make it in time. The light from the headlamps caught her, and she skidded to a stop, too petrified to keep running, too frightened to turn and face him. In her periphery, she caught sight of the little black car pulling up along the curb.

She listened to it stop, forced herself to turn, and quivered as Gino strolled out as if he had all the time in the world, swinging his gun back and forth in his hand. What would he do? Make her kneel with her hands behind her head? Shoot her execution-style? What if he abducted her again? What if they took her somewhere …

The loud blaring of a horn broke Kennedy's fear-induced paralysis, and the crumpled front end of Carl's Honda whizzed toward her. She dashed across the street, but even as she ran, she knew she wouldn't make it in time. Gino would shoot. He would kill her.

Crack.

She prayed the noise of the gun firing would wake up someone in the neighborhood. They would call the police, check the license plate, maybe get the entire scene on video.

"Get in!" Carl shouted at her, and she scurried around to the passenger side and flung open the door as another gunshot split the air around her. As soon as she was in the car, Carl slammed on the gas, and they jolted ahead.

"Buckle up." His voice was rigid. His whole body radiated tension as he leaned forward and gripped the steering wheel. "I haven't driven this fast since college."

CHAPTER 15

The Honda lurched forward, squealing ahead of Gino.

"He had a gun." Kennedy was breathing hard, her brain branded with the image of the firearm swinging low in Gino's hand.

"Take a deep breath and calm down," Carl told her. How could he talk about calm at a time like this?

"But he had a gun."

Carl swerved around a corner. "So let's be thankful we're both alive and focus on staying that way."

He yanked the steering wheel the other way, and Kennedy was thrown against her door. The wipers still smeared across the windshield.

"Sorry about that," Carl muttered.

"Do you know where this road leads?" Kennedy held onto the bottom of her seat.

Carl glanced in the rearview mirror. "Looks like we're gonna learn."

He turned down the next side street and clunked over

three speed bumps. The sound of the car's bottom scraping against the pavement zinged pain through Kennedy's ears all the way to the roots of her teeth. It was probably a ridiculous gesture, but she pushed down the lock on her door.

"Good idea." Carl did the same.

"Do you know how to get out of this neighborhood?" Kennedy asked after he turned down yet another road and sped past a school.

"If I had to guess, I'd say it's this way."

She wasn't reassured. "He's still following us," Kennedy announced, stealing a peak in the mirror.

"Yup." Carl sounded tense but not necessarily afraid. Since he was a pastor, did that mean he was more prepared to die than the average churchgoer?

They sped through a stop sign, and Kennedy clenched her jaw. She couldn't relax it even when she tried.

Carl looked both ways before swinging out of the subdivision onto the main road. "You should see if you can get a license plate number."

Kennedy turned around, expecting to be shot in the face the moment she faced Gino's car. The Honda whizzed past the streetlights so fast that they had almost a strobe effect. She could only see one or two characters at a time but figured she could rattle them off if she had to.

"Do you have your cellphone?" she asked.

"It's in my pants." Carl adjusted his weight to one hip. This was no time to be prudish. She reached into his back pocket and pulled out his little black flip-phone. Her fingers only shook a little as she dialed. Everything would be fine. She'd call the police. They'd send the squad cars to save them in a minute. Two at most.

"It's going through." She held her breath and waited for the operator's voice.

"We're sorry. All lines are busy at this time. Please hold."

It had to be some kind of joke. This wasn't customer service for some mail-order clothes catalog or online bookstore. This was serious. Life or death. And she was on hold?

"They're busy." She could hardly believe the words herself.

Carl nodded. "Must be this wind. The power's out in Medford. Our house was hit for a little bit earlier. Whole neighborhood went dark for half an hour or more."

"So people are calling 911? In the middle of the night?"

Carl was winding down one street after another, and Gino was working hard to pull up in the lane next to them.

She glanced out her window. "He's getting closer." She could see the black car in the other lane. There was no way Carl's little Honda could outrun him.

"Don't worry about Gino." Carl kept his eyes on the road.

"But he's got a gun," Kennedy reminded him. She had no idea how long Carl's old car could keep up this kind of pace and hoped the engine wouldn't give out. Were cars like horses? Could you work one until it fell over dead?

"I know." Carl's voice was calm and steady. "But he's got to focus on his driving. It's not like in the movies. You can't drive and shoot at the same time."

Kennedy hoped he was right. What would a full-time pastor know about those kinds of things, anyway? She glanced out the window right as they sped under a street lamp. The driver was scowling behind the wheel, quickly gaining on them and about to pass on the right.

"That's not Gino." Confusion slowed her mind. Her body tingled with an electric fear. "It's someone else."

The back window rolled down.

"He's in the backseat," she squealed.

"Duck!"

Kennedy could hardly hear Carl's shout over the sound of her own scream. Glass shattered on top of her as the window exploded. Shards rained down in her hair, in her eyebrows.

Kennedy screamed again as a second shot rang out.

"I'm gonna get us on Main Street. The police station's that way."

"Oh my God, oh my God." For the first time, she realized that phrase wasn't only using the Lord's name in vain. It could also be a prayer.

"Tight curve," Carl warned. He leaned into the steering wheel with his whole body, and Kennedy cried out in pain as her arm bashed against the door.

"Hallelujah!" Carl exclaimed. "We lost them!"

Kennedy glanced in the passenger mirror. The black car had missed the turn, but she only felt a slight breeze of relief because her arm was firing pain all the way down to the bone.

"You all right?" Carl asked.

Something was sticky. Something was ...

"I'm bleeding." She held up her fingers as disbelief swirled around in her gut. "I'm bleeding." She hadn't realized how terrified she was until she heard the tremor in her voice.

"From the glass?" Carl asked. His words were coated in hope that only thinly veiled his own fear.

"I'm bleeding." Her breaths became shallow. She reached up and turned on the overhead light. "I think I've been shot."

CHAPTER 16

"All right," Carl whispered. "All right."

Panic laced his voice, mirroring the panic that swelled up inside her.

"Let me just think. If I take Riverside to Governor's Ave, I can get you to the hospital. You need to apply pressure. You need to ..."

The pain hadn't been that bad until she realized what it was. The shoulder of her leather coat was torn. She couldn't even see skin beneath, just blood. What kind of diseases would infect a wound like that? She looked at her arm again, and her vision blurred.

"I don't feel too good." She had time to turn her face away from her injury before throwing up. It wasn't until her stomach was empty that she realized what she had done.

She didn't dare raise her eyes to Carl but stared at his dirty pants leg. Where was that Kleenex he had given her?

"I am so sorry," she stammered. "Here, let me help you ..."

"Don't worry about it." Carl didn't take his eyes off the road.

"I'm really, really sorry," she repeated, her fear and pain giving way to the mortification that warmed the pit of her stomach, shouting blaring accusations in her ear.

"It's ok."

She had never seen Carl so serious. Was he mad at her? Of course he was. If it hadn't been for her, he wouldn't be sitting in a smelly mess. His car wouldn't be all smashed in, and they wouldn't be fleeing for their lives. She'd be lucky if he ever spoke to her again. She'd probably have to find another church and …

"Sandy did that, too, you know."

"What?"

"When she was in labor with Jordan and I was driving her to the hospital." His voice was lighter now. A little more like normal. "Puked all over herself, the car, my arm." He let out a little chuckle. "Man, the orderly who met us at the ER, he took one look at her, went back inside, and came back with some gloves and a face mask just to help her in the doors. Can't blame the kid."

Kennedy laughed, but the jerky motion made her shoulder hurt even more.

"We're just a few minutes away from the hospital,

kiddo." Carl squeezed her knee. "You just hang tight." And then, in his comforting deep voice, Carl started to pray. He thanked God for keeping them safe and asked him to keep Gino far away from them. He prayed for the police and all those impacted by the power outages. He prayed for the doctors and nurses they would soon meet, and asked that if it was God's will they could have a chance to spread the love of Jesus to them.

He had just said "Amen" when Kennedy heard a car speeding up behind them. She turned in her seat, wincing with pain, expecting to see Gino's black vehicle.

"Oh, thank you, Lord," Carl breathed.

Kennedy never expected to be so relieved at the sight of blue and red flashing police lights. Carl pulled over and jumped out of the car, raising his arms in the air.

"Hurry!" he called, keeping both hands high. "She's been shot."

CHAPTER 17

Kennedy wanted to get out of the van, too, but there was so much glass around her she couldn't move. The police were here now. That was what really mattered. They would find Gino, put him behind bars where he belonged. Kennedy could go to her aunt's tomorrow — or was it technically today by now? When she returned to campus next month, she wouldn't have to worry about panic attacks or post-traumatic stress disorder or anything like that. Gino would face justice. So would Vinny. And she could focus on school.

Everything would return to normal, and she would be just fine.

"All right, miss, let's take a look at your arm."

A mustached policeman leaned down near Kennedy's splintered window. He shined the flashlight at her.

"Nope. That ain't glass." He straightened up, cocked his head, and muttered something into the walkie-talkie on his shoulder.

Kennedy bit her lower lip. Sure, she was in pain, but it wasn't anything the doctors couldn't handle. Nobody was freaking out about blood loss or anything like that. If her injuries were life threatening, she would know it, right? It wasn't anything like getting stabbed in the back with a four-inch blade. Her arm hurt, but what was a little pain as long as the people who wanted her dead were in custody?

Wait, they were in custody, right?

"Did you find Gino?" she asked. "The one in the black car?"

The officer lowered himself back down by the window. "Easy now. We'll have plenty of questions. But let's start by looking at that arm of yours." He frowned and mumbled something else in code on his radio. What did that mean? Did it mean she was dying? No, he'd be applying pressure if she was at risk of bleeding out, not standing there with his chin in his walkie-talkie, right?

"Did you get Gino? He's the guy they just said was another partner in the kidnapping."

"Kidnapping?" The officer shined the flashlight in Kennedy's face. "You the other girl?" he asked after a pause. "The one they picked up with Abernathy's kid?"

Kennedy nodded, and the officer let out a slow whistle

under his breath.

"All right. So this Gino just started chasing you guys in his car? What were you doing out so late?"

She wasn't sure where to start. At her chemistry final? In the subway? In her dorm room? Had that all really just happened today? Or yesterday. Why did everything get so jumbled and confusing in the middle of the night?

Kennedy gave the officer a brief rundown of her evening, starting with seeing Gino on the T.

"You were on that subway? We got word someone sabotaged it. Cut the power and set off a smoke bomb to get people freaked out."

"That must have been Gino." Even saying his name made Kennedy nauseated. Her arm throbbed. "Once we got off the T, I thought someone was following me." She didn't want to admit to the police how far she had run in the tunnel. If it really had been Gino, though, how was she still here? Wouldn't he have attacked? Maybe she started running at just the right time. Any farther down the walkway, and …

The officer frowned. "Why didn't you call the police when you recognized him?"

"I didn't know who he was. Not yet. But then I got back to my dorm, and my dad sent me the link from Channel 2 with his picture, and I recognized him then, and then my roommate did, too."

He interrupted with questions every few sentences, but eventually the entire report came out, culminating with the car chase.

"And did you get a license plate number?" He frowned again, and Kennedy wondered if he thought her whole story was a farce. Could her mind have made something like this up? She glanced at the window shards on her lap, winced as the pain deep in her arm radiated throughout her entire right side. No, this was no PTSD episode.

"I saw the license plate." She tried to recreate the image in her mind like a photograph. "I had it in my head, and then I tried calling, but you guys were busy ..."

She heard the accusatory tone in her own voice. Where had the police been when she needed them?

The officer pursed his lips together in what Kennedy guessed was some sort of approximation of a smile. "Well, if you're ever in the same situation again, try shouting the number out loud."

"What, so I don't forget?" Kennedy couldn't recall a single thought that had rushed through her brain after Gino shot through the window. How could she have remembered something as obscure as a license plate number?

"No, so we can pick it up. We were listening to you guys the entire time, you know."

"You were?"

He nodded. "Our dispatch operator got on shortly after you called. At first we thought we had a hostage situation, thought you were being forced somewhere against your will and had managed to put out a call. Then we put enough pieces together to realize you were being chased, and they sent us out after you."

"But how did you find where we were?"

"Ain't too hard if the driver names you the cross streets and tells you exactly where he's headed."

Good old Carl. So had he known? Was that why he had been naming the streets?

A female officer came up to the window. Carl followed her, and Kennedy caught the gleam in his eye as a car approaching in the opposite lane lit up his face in its headlights.

"They found the vehicle and have the suspect in custody," the officer told her partner.

Kennedy let out her breath. Everyone had something to say, even Carl, but Kennedy just sat, letting relief wash over her like water from a hot bath. The excited cacophony was interrupted by the siren of an ambulance speeding toward them.

"Good." The policeman leaned down. "EMTs are here. They'll get you fixed up just fine."

CHAPTER 18

Two men rushed to Kennedy's window and started shouting questions at her.

"Can you breathe?"

"Are you able to move your fingers?"

"Do you hurt anywhere near your neck or back?"

She wished they'd just get her cleaned up and let her get some rest, but they kept up the barrage for five minutes or longer.

"All right," one of them said. "We'll get you on the stretcher and take you to the hospital. Won't take long. We're just a few miles away."

"I can walk without a stretcher."

He looked at her dubiously.

"Really," she insisted. "I'm fine." She unbuckled her seatbelt to prove her point.

"No, don't do that, miss." He held out his hand.

She ignored the gesture. "I'm all right. I don't need a stretcher."

He gave a little shrug. "Ok." He turned and called to the other EMT, "Leave it there. She's gonna walk."

"You sure?" he called back.

Why did everyone treat her like a fragile china doll about to shatter?

She swept some glass chunks off her lap and held onto the car door to raise herself to her feet. The world spun for a second or two and then settled down again. She smiled at the EMT. "See?"

He shrugged. "All right. This way." He gestured toward the ambulance.

"Doesn't that seem a little overkill?" she asked. "Carl could drive me in his car."

He turned and eyed the maroon mess. "That thing? Does it still run?"

"It got us this far."

"Well, we really need you in the ambulance. We have some paperwork to go over on the ride."

Kennedy didn't argue anymore. The sooner she complied, the sooner this whole ordeal would be over. She walked herself to the back of the ambulance and eyed the gurney, thankful she wasn't so injured she needed something like that.

Her shoulder smarted a little as she hoisted herself into

the back and sat in one of the seats along the side.

The paramedic cleared his throat. "Actually, we're gonna need you on the stretcher."

"You're kidding, right?"

He shook his head. "Standard policy. It's got the best straps. Safer than the seats." He walked over and propped up the back. "If it makes you feel better, you don't have to lie down."

He was just doing his job, Kennedy had to keep reminding herself. She felt about as useless as a discarded Petri dish as he strapped her down. It was all right. Before long she'd be asleep in a nice bed.

"How you doing, sweetheart?" Carl stepped onto the ambulance platform and gave her a paternal smile.

"I'll be fine."

"You need anything?" he asked. "Want to call your mom? What time is it over there, anyway? Think she'd be awake?"

The last thing Kennedy needed was for Carl to call her parents back in Yanji and freak them out. She'd fill them in once things quieted down. "No thanks." She tried to smile, remembering she was the one guilty of ruining Carl's whole evening.

The paramedic took a step toward Carl. "You're

welcome to follow us to the hospital, but we're ready to roll out, so I'll need you to hop down."

Carl folded his arms across his chest and stared at the man. "She is not going out of my sight."

He frowned. "I'm sorry. We only transport immediate family. And I, uh … well, you, um … You're not actually related, are you?" He glanced nervously from Kennedy with her pale-white skin to Carl's dark complexion. If she hadn't just been shot in the arm, Kennedy might have enjoyed watching his discomfort.

Carl took a step forward, puffing out his chest to hint at the kind of beast he must have been in his football days. "You don't think I could be her father?"

The paramedic eyed Kennedy once more. "He's your dad?"

Kennedy just wanted to get to the hospital. She didn't care if Carl came with her or followed in his car. None of that mattered. She just wanted to get her injury taken care of, and then she wanted to sleep for a very long time.

"Sir?" The policewoman came up and addressed Carl. "We still have a few more questions, and then you'll be on your way."

"She's not going out of my sight," Carl repeated.

The officer took a breath, glanced at Carl's hard-set

face, and sighed. "We'll caravan, then. You follow the ambulance. We'll be right behind you."

Carl nodded. "Good. Because there are men out there who are ready to break every law in the book to keep her from testifying against them. She's not going into that hospital without an armed escort. Whoever wanted her dead might guess she was shot. Hospital would be the first place they'd look for her."

"Wait a minute," Kennedy inserted. Had she heard them right? Was the exhaustion making her brain fuzzy? Or perhaps it was the blood loss. She hadn't thought she had been wounded that seriously. "You said you had Gino in custody."

The policewoman frowned at Carl and then turned to Kennedy with a sigh. "We caught the driver. Unfortunately, he didn't fit the description of the suspect we're looking for."

Carl put his hand on Kennedy's stretcher. "They've got patrols out looking for Gino right now. He's probably on foot. Trust me. He's not gonna get far."

Blood drained from Kennedy's face and mingled with the bile in her gut. She wasn't going to dwell on Gino right now. What was it about positive thinking having healing powers? Hadn't she read an article like that in her psychology class? Or was it something her roommate had said? It sounded like something Willow would dream up.

Carl held Kennedy's gaze. "I'll be right behind you guys. You all right with that?" he asked.

Kennedy nodded even though she was too tired to try to smile. "That sounds fine."

After he hopped down, the paramedic swung the two doors shut. He glanced at Kennedy once and then back at his own hands after he buckled himself in. "So, wait, he's not really your dad, then, is he?"

Kennedy shook her head. "No. He's my pastor."

The young man's cheeks flushed red, and the ambulance sped off to the whining of its own sirens.

CHAPTER 19

Kennedy wished the doctors and nurses believed her when she told them she was all right. She wasn't even bleeding anymore. Why couldn't they just clean her up, tape on a massive Band-Aid, knock her up with painkillers, and let her go to sleep?

A team of a dozen or more nurses met her as soon as the paramedics wheeled her into the back doors of the ER. One shoved a stethoscope to her chest. Another clipped a plastic clamp to her pointer finger. People were shouting, running. She felt like she was on an old episode of one of those medical dramas her mom watched.

She tried to look back to see if Carl was there, but a nurse reached down and pinned her on the stretcher.

They sped her to a little room separated from the main hall by a hanging curtain. A doctor in full gear snapped on his second blue glove when they wheeled her in.

"All right." He gestured at one of the nurses. "Let's cut that coat off her."

"What?" Kennedy tried to sit up, but the same nurse held her down once more.

Another nurse reached into her pocket and pulled out a pair of scissors with a little metal ball at the end.

"Not sure how these will work." She held up Kennedy's sleeve.

"You can't cut my coat," Kennedy insisted. "It was from my dad."

"You know it's ruined already, right?"

Kennedy bit her lip while the nurse sliced away at her early Christmas present. It didn't matter, she told herself. She just wanted to get this whole ER visit over with.

"Oh, look at that."

She didn't understand the nurse's tone. Why did she say it that way?

"That's all?" another asked.

"Probably could have saved the coat."

Hadn't Kennedy tried to tell them?

The doctor gave a few orders, and everyone left except for the nurse with the scissors.

Just doing her job, Kennedy repeated to herself over and over.

"Well, looks fine to me." The doctor also stood up. "Dolores here will clean you up, and then when the police are done with whatever questions they've got, I have no reason to keep you here."

He left without any sort of good-bye. Kennedy didn't even get the chance to thank him.

Dolores set to work, spraying her wound with a big can of saline and spreading a large blob of antibiotic ointment. The area burned hot, but the pain was bearable. Nothing like when she was in the hospital last fall.

"So, you a student around here?" Dolores asked.

"Yeah." Kennedy didn't necessarily like telling people she went to Harvard. That kind of confession automatically made certain people assume she was a preppy rich kid.

Dolores kept her eyes on the wound and opened a package of sterile gauze. "Whatcha studying?"

"I'm pre-med." It sounded silly to mention here. Right now, Kennedy didn't even have the know-how to clean a wound like hers.

Dolores frowned and muttered, "That'll pay the bills."

Kennedy didn't say anything. This wasn't the first time someone had mentioned money when they found out she planned to become a doctor. She wasn't sure how much she believed the common perception that every MD was filthy rich. With all the student loans she was accumulating, she wondered if she'd have enough disposable income to buy her own white coat once she finally graduated med school.

Dolores was wrapping some brown stretchy cloth around the gauze when someone pulled back the curtain.

"Here she is."

She immediately recognized Carl's voice. She had been wondering if they would let him back here. Behind him was Detective Drisklay with his salt and pepper beard and coarse mustache.

"So, I guess our ten o'clock meeting got moved up a few hours." He took a drink from a steaming Styrofoam cup, and Kennedy recognized the scent of coffee that followed him wherever he went. She wasn't sure if he was in a good mood or not. She had never seen him either happy or sad and wondered if he even had an emotional life to speak of. "Well, since we're both here, I've got a few questions for you." He sat down on the doctor's swivel chair and whipped out a notepad.

Dolores finished her work and excused herself with a promise to come back with painkillers and Kennedy's discharge papers. Carl crossed his arms impassively by the curtain, reminding Kennedy of her childhood pet schnauzer when he tried to act territorial. Tonight might turn into an amusing memory when she looked back on it, but right now all she hoped was to stay awake to answer whatever questions Drisklay had for her.

"So, they tell me the wound was pretty superficial."

Kennedy nodded. "Just a graze."

He frowned. "You're lucky, then."

She wondered what history lay behind his hardened gaze.

"How long have you known Gino?"

"I just met him tonight. I mean, I never met him. He was just there chasing us. Oh, and before that he was on the subway."

The detective frowned and didn't write anything.

Kennedy decided to order her thoughts more logically. "I didn't know who he was until tonight. I didn't even know there was another partner involved. I saw the news before I went to bed, and then I realized I had seen him on the T earlier. Green Line."

"Which branch?"

Kennedy had a hard time keeping all the different lines straight. "Whichever one goes to the Opera House."

Detective Drisklay frowned. "That would be E."

She nodded. "E, then."

"Inbound or outbound?"

"We were headed back to campus."

"Inbound." He scribbled a little more. "And you hadn't seen him before then?"

Kennedy stopped herself from shaking her head too soon. Hadn't the man looked familiar on the T? Or was that just her memory playing tricks on her? How did witnesses in crime novels keep such great track of faces and details?

"I think he looked a little familiar, but I can't be sure."

Detective Drisklay kept his pen poised over his notebook. "So you've had previous encounters with him? Did you see him working with Vinny?"

As hard as she tried to forget everything that happened to her last fall, she couldn't get Vinny's face out of her mind. She sometimes replayed whole segments of her captivity at a time, as if a big projector screen took over her brain and went over every minute detail. She was certain she hadn't seen Gino with them.

"No, he wasn't there." She frowned. Where had she seen his face? Maybe her memories were jumbled. Maybe she really hadn't recognized him on the T. None of it made sense.

"He had a scar." Detective Drisklay rolled back his sleeve and drew an imaginary line from his thumb down past his wrist. "Here on the right hand. Ring any bells?"

Kennedy frowned. Maybe if she had more sleep …

"Well, if you remember, we'll come back to it." Drisklay flipped a page in his notebook.

If Drisklay was anything, he was thorough. Eventually Dolores poked her head in, handed Kennedy a huge pill and a miniature Dixie cup of water, and sneaked back out. Carl even left his station at the curtain to sit down in one of the hard plastic chairs lining the wall. He didn't exactly doze, but every once in a while, Kennedy caught his eyes glossing over right before he shook his head and jerked himself back to attention.

Drisklay picked Kennedy's brain completely clean of every detail from the past twenty-four hours. Finally, he took the last long swig of coffee, which must have been room temperature by now, and stood up. "I appreciate you taking the time to see me."

It wasn't as though Kennedy had much of a choice, but she returned what she hoped was a polite smile. Where was Dolores? She was ready for those discharge papers so she could leave.

Drisklay pulled on a pair of black winter gloves. "By the way, we've got men out looking for Gino now, but we're making provisions for your security after your discharge."

Carl leaned forward in his seat. "What exactly does that mean?"

"I understand Miss Stern will be sleeping at your house."

Carl nodded. "That's right."

"We're going to send out a car, maybe two, to keep watch at your place tonight."

Carl let out a sigh. "Well, then, I'll give you my address."

The detective patted his pocket. "Already got it. The men are on their way there now making everything secure."

Carl's whole upper body tensed. "I got my wife at home."

Drisklay gave a respectful nod. "They don't need to go in or wake her up or bother your wife at all. They'll just walk around the premises, make sure any entrances are secure."

Carl glanced nervously at his watch. "Maybe I should call her." He stood up and excused himself.

Drisklay turned his attention back to Kennedy. "As for you, I imagine you'll want to sleep in tomorrow instead of coming downtown like we planned."

Kennedy was too tired to do anything but nod.

"That's fine. I'll call you around noon."

"I'm supposed to fly to my aunt's at four. Is that going to be a problem?"

Drisklay frowned and buttoned up his coat. "We'll talk about that tomorrow."

Kennedy tried to ignore his ominous tone.

A young nurse in Betty Boop scrubs popped in almost as soon as the detective left. "I've got your discharge instructions." Her voice was far too chipper for this time of day. Night. Whatever it was. She gave Kennedy a big grin. "My guess is someone's ready to go home, huh?"

CHAPTER 20

"How are you holding up, kiddo?" Carl certainly looked different behind the wheel of his Honda when they weren't getting gunned down by a crazed criminal.

"I'm exhausted." Kennedy shut her eyes. All the nurse had given her after the horse pill was some directions about changing the bandages.

"Well, the good news is we'll be home soon. And just so you know, Sandy's probably still awake," he warned. "She'll want to see for herself that you're well taken care of."

Kennedy was glad for the warning. If Carl's wife was awake, it would take ten or twenty minutes at minimum to tell the entire story over tea, but Kennedy could handle that. The Lindgrens were about as close a thing to family as Kennedy had in Cambridge, and Christmas season was a lousy time to be alone. At least Drisklay didn't need her downtown tomorrow morning so she could sleep in.

Kennedy kept checking the rear-view mirror, and she caught Carl doing the same on more than one occasion.

"You'd think we're a bunch of loons," Carl joked when they both glanced up at the same time. "Throwing glances over our shoulders every chance we get."

It felt good to laugh even about something as dangerous as a murderous stalker. Kennedy kept reminding herself about the officers Drisklay had promised to send to the Lindgrens' house. Nothing was going to happen tonight.

When they got to Carl and Sandy's, the police car was already out front. Carl opened the garage door but stopped in the driveway and lowered his window when a tall officer headed over. The man kept one hand on his belt and walked over in that special slow gait Kennedy had previously assumed was just for cops in movies.

"Mr. Lindgren." He nodded at them both through the window. "Miss Stern."

"Thanks for being here." Carl held his hand out.

The officer didn't make eye contact but kept scanning the whole perimeter while he shook Carl's hand. "We don't want to bother you any. We already took a look around. We'll be the first to know if anyone tries something funny."

Carl nodded. "I appreciate that. I'll just pull in the car then."

"Yup," the policeman replied. "You just go about your night like normal and try to forget we're here."

Carl rolled his window halfway up and paused. "Oh, if we run into problems, do we call you or 911?"

The officer lowered his gaze as well as his voice. "If you run into problems, we'll know it before you even have a chance to yell."

The answer wasn't as reassuring as Kennedy might have hoped. Still, she was thankful to be home, or at least some semblance of it. Anywhere safe with a bed was good enough for her.

Carl pulled the Honda slowly into the garage and then came around to help Kennedy out of the car. She could walk just fine on her own, but she didn't mind having Carl to lean on. Something about his closeness was reassuring. He escorted her up the garage steps and into the kitchen, where the hot smell of cinnamon and vanilla mingled together and set her mouth watering.

"It's about time you showed up!" Sandy exclaimed, wiping her floury hands on her apron. "Those men outside were making me nervous."

"Just remember they're here to keep us safe." Carl gave

her a peck on the cheek.

"I know." Sandy waved a spatula in the air. "But it still gives me willies."

He reached out and rubbed the back of her neck.

"Kennedy," she asked, hardly noticing his affections, "do you feel up for some cookies and milk? I have tea, too, if you'd prefer. Oh, and these cinnamon rolls are fresh. I made them this morning."

A few minutes later, they were all seated at the dining room table with fresh desserts and mugs of hot, steaming tea. Kennedy put an extra spoonful of sugar in hers, figuring she deserved it after a night like this. In the background, the Lindgrens' radio crooned about a white Christmas, and the wind howled outside.

"Any more problems with the electricity while we were gone?" Carl asked.

Sandy took a sip of tea. "No, thank the Lord. Only that little episode before you left. I unplugged the TV, though, just in case."

Carl leaned back in his chair, and Kennedy wondered how he could be so calm. Didn't he remember everything they had gone through? Gino had tried to kill them. They would be dead right now if it hadn't been for a major dose of luck.

No, not luck, Kennedy had to remind herself. Had she even bothered to thank the Lord for bringing her through a night like this?

Sandy asked Kennedy about her semester and her finals, and Kennedy was grateful she didn't have to talk about Gino or tonight's excitement. After a little more small talk and two more cookies, music from *The Nutcracker* faded in on the Lindgrens' radio, and Kennedy strained to remember if it had really been tonight she had gone to the ballet with Reuben. She sure would have a lot to tell him when she returned to campus in January.

"Oh, you got Justice's old spot, didn't you?" Sandy pointed to the numerous nicks in the wood. "That boy would fidget with his knife the whole meal through. It's a wonder he ever grew. Boy hardly ate a thing."

"How many kids do you guys have?" Kennedy asked. When Carl led her parents' church back in New York, she remembered the Lindgrens having a large family, but she could never keep track of how many there were.

Carl and Sandy exchanged frowns and both gave different answers at the same time.

"Thirteen."

"Six."

They chuckled, and Sandy reached over to pat

Kennedy's arm. "We did foster care, and then we adopted some at different ages."

"The correct answer," Carl answered with his mouth stuffed with cinnamon roll, "is three biological, three adopted, and a whole lot of other sons and daughters of the heart, even if the state doesn't recognize them."

"Well, and some of them wouldn't claim us anymore, either," Sandy added, taking a sip of tea.

Kennedy looked from one to the other but could only guess at the chaos, the heartache, the drama, the fullness, the joy that had been the Lindgrens' family life. She wondered if either one would say any more, but they were both staring at their plates quietly. Had Kennedy said something wrong? Had she opened old wounds?

"And how many grandkids?" she finally asked. Wasn't that a subject grandparents loved to talk about? She remembered Pastor Carl's office, all the hand-drawn pictures and professional portraits he had up of his grandchildren.

"Five," he mumbled into his mug.

Sandy raised her eyes to meet Kennedy's. "Six," she corrected softly. "Five here with us, and one little one with the angels in heaven."

Carl took a loud gulp of coffee and clunked his mug on the table. "That was delicious, dear." He scooted his chair back noisily and kissed Sandy on top of her head. "It's been a long night."

Kennedy frowned. Why was he leaving so abruptly?

Sandy took his hand in hers, and a tender look passed between them. "You sure?"

His face softened. "You know me, baby. I get grumpy without my beauty rest." He gave a little wink and kissed his wife once more. "Love you."

Sandy pecked his hand before letting it go. "I won't be long."

"Yes, you will," he laughed. "Just don't keep Kennedy up. Remember, she's had the hardest day of all of us."

"I'll behave myself," Sandy promised and blew him a kiss.

The floorboards creaked under Carl's weight as he shuffled down the hall.

Kennedy stared into her plate, uncertain what she had done to make Carl leave. "I'm really sorry." She kept her voice low so he wouldn't overhear. "I didn't realize ..."

"Of course you didn't, sweetie." Sandy stood and brought the platter of cookies over to the table. She set two more in front of Kennedy without asking. "Of course you didn't." Sandy swept her hair over her shoulder and sat down with a sigh. "Have I ever told you about our daughter, Blessing?"

CHAPTER 21

"Carl was doing campus ministry when we met," Sandy began. "Anyway, we got married and knew right away we would have a big family. We just figured between us and the Lord we had plenty of love to share, and that's what we wanted to do.

"So our first two kids were born while Carl was serving as a campus minister, and our youngest came when his daddy was just starting seminary. Well, like I said, we thought we'd keep on having more and more, but I had some complications delivering Justice. Pretty major ones, actually. So we knew God had closed the door for us, at least biologically speaking.

"Well, it was right around that time when I read a report about Romania and the orphans there, and I showed it to Carl, and we both decided that was the next step for our family. We wanted to do everything just right. I talked with some folks who had adopted from overseas, read up on the subject. Prayed our heads off. I still remember the day I walked the kids to the post office to mail out our application packet. I was more nervous than I had been on my wedding day. And I was talking to the kids — they were still little, but we talked about it all the time. Talked to them about how we could open our home to a new brother or a new sister, and they had so many questions, and our little girl Bridget wanted to know what orphanage *she* had come from, which of course led to all kinds of interesting discussions."

Sandy smiled at the memory. "And then we waited."

Kennedy remembered how hard it was waiting to hear back from all the colleges she applied to. That had been torturous enough.

"Three weeks later, we got our notice in the mail." Sandy glanced down at the table and ran her napkin over an imaginary smudge. "The adoption agency declined our application. Romania wasn't open for interracial couples to adopt."

Kennedy leaned forward in her seat. "What? That's ridiculous."

Sandy shook her head slowly. "The sad thing was, after all we had been through already, neither of us were that surprised. Disappointed … absolutely. Felt like one of our children was stolen. But surprised? Well, let's just say Carl and I had seen a lot worse by then."

"Like what?" Kennedy had studied the American Civil Rights movement in high school, but it always felt like any other period of history — long-ago events that only historians and a few great-grandparents remembered or cared about. She counted back the decades. Had Carl and Sandy lived through that tumultuous mess?

Sandy sighed loudly. "Oh, it's no secret what we've been through. But it's not necessarily the happiest of subjects."

Kennedy took the hint and tried to remember how the conversation had turned down this depressing rabbit-trail in the first place. "Well, what about your daughter?" she asked. "Blessing, you said her name was?"

A smile shined through the darkness that had obscured Sandy's face. "That's right. Blessing. See, after the whole Romania incident, we stopped thinking about formal adoptions. We figured until the world was ready to give us the same parental rights they gave any other adoptive family, well, we weren't going to put ourselves out there to get hurt dozens of times all over again." She chuckled. "So we became foster parents."

Kennedy didn't know what was so funny about the remark but offered a little smile.

"Well, that first year I forget just how many kids we had. See, some were through the system, but then others heard we had an open-door policy, and boy, did we see some beautiful children those first years. Our own kids loved it. They were all little social bugs. All loved having temporary brothers and sisters to live and play with. Always cried when they left. All of us did."

She glanced down the hallway at the long rows of photographs before continuing. "Anyway, like I said, at that point we weren't looking into formal adoption. We just figured the Lord would send us the kids that needed a home, and we'd take care of them for however long God needed us to. Well, it wasn't as easy as all that. Politics, CPS, ugly custody battles ..."

Her voice trailed off. Kennedy didn't know much about the foster system but sensed it must be trying to bring in kids like that, never knowing how long they'd stay, never knowing what kind of baggage they carried with them.

"Anyway, we got Blessing when she was twelve years old. We had just started the Redemption Temple church plant in New York at that point. Times weren't easy, and money was especially tight that year, but we got the call and knew we had to take her in. Her mom had been out of the picture for years. Dad had never been in the picture from as far as we knew. Wasn't even listed on the birth certificate. She had been living with her grandma somewhere upstate, and from what we could gather, her grandma was a decent, God-fearing sort. Well, when she died, Blessing got passed from one relative to the next. Happens so often. And let's just say that being someone's aunt or uncle or step-dad's ex-sister-in-law doesn't make you qualified to be a guardian. By the time we got Blessing, she was so broken. So broken, so hurt …"

Sandy stuck out her finger to touch a cinnamon roll. She made a comment about them getting cold and would have gotten up to reheat them if Kennedy hadn't declined multiple offers for seconds.

"Anyway," Sandy went on after Kennedy finally convinced her she was full, "she came to us, and we knew she was ours. Not that we didn't love the other foster kids who came to us. We did, and even if I say so myself, I think we did right by most of them. But Blessing was different. We knew — just as sure as we knew Bridget and Jordan and Justice were ours — that Blessing belonged in our family.

"It didn't happen right away, and later we realized how lucky we were that it happened at all, but we adopted Blessing when she was fourteen. She was a lively little thing. Lively and headstrong and stubborn, and we loved her to death. She had some problems with the church youth group. Said she thought the people there treated her like a charity project instead of a person, and looking back, I think she was probably right. I think there were things we could have done differently for her if we had really known. But none of us understand these things going into it, right?"

Kennedy nodded even though she had never been in an even remotely similar situation. The closest experience she had with guardianship was when her friend in high school asked her to watch over her fruit fly specimens in the lab while her family went on vacation to Germany for a week.

Sandy poured more tea into both their mugs before continuing. "Well, when she was sixteen, she ran away. We hadn't been fighting. There weren't any boyfriends, not that we knew of. She just had the heart of a runaway. We looked and looked. Redemption Temple even gave Carl a three-month sabbatical. We went everywhere. When we finished searching the city, we went up and down the East Coast, following leads, not finding anything. It was Carl who did most of the travelling, actually. I had to stay home with the other kids. We had adopted another little boy by then from the foster system as well, and we just couldn't uproot everyone to go looking in crack holes, if you'll pardon my language."

Kennedy had to take a sip of tea to hide her bemused smile.

"We finally found her right under our noses in Manhattan. With the exact same uncle who was the reason she finally ended up in foster care in the first place. They were both homeless, living in some kind of tent neighborhood somewhere near Alphabet City. Carl never told me all the details. They were too gruesome. He knew as her mom I just couldn't handle them all.

"She was strung out. Addicted to all kinds of street drugs. God knows how she and that uncle of hers were supporting their habits. I have my guesses, of course, but there are some things better not asked. So Carl found her, but he didn't drag her home. He didn't beat up the uncle, but God knows he deserved it. He just asked her, 'Sweetie, d'you wanna come home?' Simple as that. He'd been a pastor for quite some time now, and he knew a thing or two about those kind of addictions and how they work. You don't just save someone who's not ready to be saved."

Sandy stirred her tea while she spoke. "And Blessing told him no. No, she didn't want to go home. Didn't want to go back to the rules and the snobby youth group kids and the stuffy church where she was expected to act like a perfect pastor's kid. Redemption Temple was like that back then. I don't know if you remember very well. Really, I would have felt the same way probably if I had been in her shoes. So Carl told her, 'We love you, we're glad to know you're safe, and would you mind giving us a call maybe once a month or so just so we don't get too worried?'

"So he came home, and I have to tell you I wasn't as level-headed about the whole thing as my husband. I resented him, truth be told. Back then I didn't understand why he didn't just drag her home. She was our daughter. She belonged with us. It wasn't a pretty time in our marriage."

Kennedy had a hard time picturing the Lindgrens really struggling in that area. For as long as she had known them, they were affectionate and doting, much more romantic than her own parents ever were.

"Well," Sandy continued, "I finally decided all I could do was pray. We needed Carl back home, and the church needed its pastor again. So that's what I did. I prayed. I know it never came close to what Christ suffered, but I think I've got a little more appreciation for what Jesus went through in Gethsemane after that season. A few months later, there she was, there on our doorstep, looking sad and timid and scared. Just like the prodigal, only I hadn't seen her coming at a distance or I would have hitched up my skirt and ran to her just like in the story.

"She didn't say much. We didn't ask much, not at first, at least. We were just glad to be a family again. She had to detox. I've never seen a soul suffer like that, not in my entire life. There's no explaining it, especially when it's your own daughter there, fighting her demons. And when I say demons, I mean demons. 'Course I could pray for her, help the battle that way, but the struggle really was hers. I couldn't go there with her. I would have, though. Carl and I both, we both would have traded spots with her in a heartbeat had God allowed it. But he has his reasons.

"She stayed clean the first time about four months, if I remember right. And then it was just repeat, the whole thing all over again. The disappearing. The looking, except this time Carl couldn't take time off work. The waiting. Each time the phone rings, we think it's the police calling to ask us to identify our baby girl's body in a morgue."

Sandy's voice caught, and she inhaled the steam from her tea.

"And then she'd come home, always more broken than the last time. The detoxes were just as awful, just as soul-wrenching to watch, but it was easier now for her to go back. Easier to relapse. But it was easier to find her, too.

She always ended up with the same crowd. Same bad-news uncle. Same sad story all over again."

Kennedy didn't know what to say. It made everything she suffered during her first semester of college sound like a carousel ride.

"Well, I'm probably making it out a lot more awful than it was, but really there were good times, too. When she was clean, she was great to be with. Good company for me. We were taking in a lot of medically-fragile babies back then, and I honestly don't know how I could have survived without her smiles. She'd get up early to make my morning tea, and we'd have a few minutes together quiet before the babies woke up. But all it took was one trigger, one bad day, one phone call from an old friend, and she'd be out of our lives for months.

"We did everything we could think of. We tackled the problem from every angle. Took her to counseling. Took her to a deliverance ministry team from a church in Waltham. Sent her for eight months to a Christian girls' home in Vermont. That's probably the longest she stayed clean.

"It was when she was in Vermont that she wrote to tell us the real reason she ran away that first time. She was pregnant, just some boy at school Carl had warned her to stay away from, but she hadn't listened. And she was scared of what those church ladies would say, and looking back at how the women of Redemption Temple used to be, well, I don't blame her. And so instead of taking the problem to Carl and me, she ran off and took care of it herself. Thought she found the easy fix, but she was scarred. So scarred.

"That's how Carl and I got involved in pro-life ministry, actually. We wanted to understand what Blessing was going through. We really did. Back then, people didn't talk about things like post-abortive syndrome. I had never heard the phrase. But we realized if Blessing was suffering something that awful, how many other girls were, too? And then, we got to thinking, we were really grieving that baby we lost. It wasn't just Blessing who lost a child. We lost a grandbaby, too. Our first grandbaby. A grandbaby we would have loved and cared for and even helped raise if Blessing had just asked us. And we were grieving, which got us thinking that other moms and dads and grandmas and grandpas were probably going through the same thing.

"That girls' home in Vermont was really good for her. Taught her to take responsibility for her own actions, but they also helped her find healing from some of the things in her past. Things that had happened to her early on that no child made in God's image should ever have to endure. Really good folks. We still support the ministry there. That's how highly we think of them. Anyway, she almost made a whole year in Vermont before she crashed, but when she finally did, it was worse than all the other times combined. Reminds me of that story of the demon who leaves a house and then returns with seven other friends, all stronger than the first. We went a few years not even knowing if she was alive. She was twenty before we heard from her again."

Kennedy shook her head. No wonder her own dad freaked out so much at the thought of sending her off to college alone. "What's she doing now?"

Sandy smiled. "She's living in Boston. Got a job at a bank. Been working steady there for four or five years now. Just got promoted last fall. She's the assistant branch manager, or something like that. She's dating a nice young man. They're living together, but I told Carl after all she's gone through, we're not going to make a big deal about that. She's got a little boy. He's five. I watch him three days a week." Sandy leaned over and pointed down the hall. "That's his picture right there. First one in the middle row."

Kennedy smiled at the portrait of a precocious-looking

youngster in a three-piece suit. He had his hand on his hip and a smirk on his face that yelled mischief. Kennedy guessed he kept Sandy's hands plenty full when he was over.

"He's a sassy one," Sandy mused. "Spoiled, too, but bright as a lightbulb."

Kennedy looked down the long hallway of photos, wondering how many other stories lay behind each one. She was about to ask how many foster kids they had taken in all together when Carl's voice boomed from the back room. "Princess, you need to let that poor, exhausted child get her sleep."

Sandy pouted. "I suppose he's right. You're probably tired, aren't you? Ready for bed?"

"I think that sounds like a good idea."

Sandy scooted her chair back. "You know where the guest room is. I left a nightgown in there if you want and a dress you can wear in the morning. It's loose. It shouldn't bother your bandage one bit."

"I really appreciate everything you've done."

Sandy waved her hand in the air and made a little *pshaw* sound. "Don't mention it. Oh, I should have asked you earlier. Do you want me to find you a toothbrush?"

All Kennedy wanted to do now was sleep. "It'll be all

right for just the night."

"You sure?" Sandy put her hand on her hip and eyed the empty plate. "That was a lot of sugar."

"Yeah, I just don't want you to worry about ..."

Before Kennedy could complete her thought, Sandy was two steps down the hall. "No trouble at all, sweetie. Just stay there. It won't take me more than a minute."

Kennedy slumped down in her chair, figuring she could probably fall asleep right there if Sandy took too long. She always knew there was something special about the Lindgrens' home. Every time they had her over for dinner, or when she had spent a long weekend here recovering from her injuries last fall, she had noticed its peaceful, welcoming feel. At the time, Kennedy thought it was just because she was so homesick, and the Lindgrens were the only people she knew before arriving at college. Now she wondered if there was something more to it, if Carl and Sandy's generous and hospitable spirits just made the place seem inviting to everyone who came in. A house with spare toiletries just in case someone needed a place to stay.

Sandy padded down the hall, holding out a toothbrush and travel-size tube of toothpaste. "Here you go, sweetie. I told you it wouldn't take long."

CHAPTER 22

Sandy gave a good-night hug. Kennedy wouldn't have been totally surprised if she had offered to tuck her in bed. Kennedy went to the bathroom to brush her teeth and heard Sandy padding down the hall in her fuzzy slippers. She felt like she was already sleepwalking by the time she made it to the Lindgrens' back room. They kept the bed ready at all times, day or night, to welcome the tired and needy. Kennedy wondered how many others besides herself had found shelter here in this past year alone.

It was late. Kennedy shut her eyes. She didn't even have the energy to change into Sandy's nightgown. All she wanted was to sleep. To sleep and forget that tonight had ever happened. She would do things so differently if she had a chance to start her college career over again. So differently. She had flown to the States with so many plans. So many expectations of what her college experience would be like and what she'd get out of it. Her high-school self had fantasized about meeting a boy, falling in love. She had quickly discovered there simply wasn't time for romance, not for a pre-med student like her. Reuben was the closest thing she had to a ...

No, she didn't want to think like that. He was such a good friend. So encouraging. So fun. His humor and easy ways made him the perfect juxtaposition to her uptight personality, which is why they got along so well in the lab. He was a great study partner. A great friend, really. And she didn't want to ruin that by dwelling on ...

She snuggled under the blankets but couldn't lie on her right side. Her arm wasn't throbbing anymore, but it still smarted when she adjusted her position, as if the skin was being stretched too far apart near the wounded area. If she could just get to sleep, her body would forget about the pain. She could spend hours in blissful delirium.

It was so quiet here compared to the Harvard dorm. No students stomping by. No voices in the hall. No music or shouting from the other rooms. Kennedy thought back over her first semester. Academically speaking, everything had gone pretty well. Everything except her chemistry final, at least. The only class she wasn't totally sure about was calculus, but most of that was her TA's fault, since he expected her to show her work a different way than she had learned in high school.

Harvard hadn't been exactly what she expected. She figured a school like that would have a large Christian group, but she only went to one worship gathering early in September. The songs were all unfamiliar, and none of the students introduced themselves to her. She hadn't gotten very well plugged in to Carl's church, either, but part of that was her own fault. Sundays were just so busy with study groups and lab write-ups and catching up for her literature classes. That didn't mean she wasn't making time for God, though, did it?

Was that why she was still having a hard time getting over everything? Was it because she hadn't been as faithful going to church as she should? St. Margaret's was just so different from what she was used to back at her parents' home. Each time she got back to campus after going to Carl's church, she had to sit and read for an hour or two just to unwind. It was like sensory overload, with the loud music and the dancing video screen. And so many people. How could anyone even get to know anybody at a church that size?

Still, a command is a command. Maybe that's why she was still struggling so much. She had gotten really consistent with her prayer and Bible study, which made her wonder why God still hadn't taken her problems away.

Was God waiting to heal her — to help her truly forget the trauma of last fall — until she made church attendance a higher priority?

Well, if that's what it took, she'd be there every week without fail. She just wanted to move on.

Her arm ached. She didn't know if the horse pill from the ER was wearing off, or if her conversation with Sandy had been enough of a distraction to keep her from the discomfort. She should be thankful. It was a minor wound as far as bullet injuries go. That didn't take away the burning though, the smarting that throbbed and radiated throughout her whole upper body. Pain seeped through her veins all the way to her spine. No matter which way she turned in bed, she couldn't ease the sting.

Tylenol, maybe? The nurse told her she could take some over the next few days for the pain, but Kennedy hadn't thought to ask how soon she could take one after swallowing that monstrous tablet in the ER. She had assumed she would get to the Lindgrens' and sleep straight through the night. Well, the nurse hadn't advised her against taking something.

She sat and rubbed her eyes to clear her fuzzy vision. She was dizzy. Why couldn't her body just relax? She hated to think of bothering the Lindgrens, but she needed something to help her sleep. Maybe they kept something in the medicine cabinet. Her legs were heavy as she walked to the bathroom. It felt as if the night would never end. She was thankful for the food and warm tea in her belly, but she would have preferred it if her dad hadn't called her back at her dorm in the first place, if Gino had never found out where she was, if none of this had happened at all.

She imagined telling Reuben about it over pizza and Coke in the student union. It would be old news by the time she saw him again. Maybe she'd even relate the whole story without shaking.

She rummaged quietly in the bathroom cupboards, wishing for a robe or extra blanket to ward off the winter chill that hung all around her like condensation on a lab flask. No medicine there. The kitchen, maybe? She sneaked down the hall, unwilling to bother Carl and Sandy, and looked at the microwave clock. Not quite three in the morning. What was she doing awake? Even her busiest nights studying for a test or finishing off a research paper on campus almost always saw her in bed by this time. Exhaustion clouded around her head like a thick New England fog, but she was also jumpy, as if she had gone to bed after drinking a full cup of coffee. Was it something in the medicine from the ER? The stress of the night? The danger that lurked in the dark corners of the Lindgrens' house?

She pulled back the blinds of the kitchen window. The police car was still parked out front. She couldn't see the men inside, but took comfort knowing they were there. Nothing could hurt her now. Nothing could get her here.

"Stop right where you are, or I'll shoot."

The words chilled Kennedy's blood. The back of her neck tingled as she turned slowly around.

"Kennedy?"

The surprised look on her pastor's face might have made Kennedy laugh if he hadn't been pointing a gun at her. He quickly lowered the weapon.

"I'm sorry," he was stammering.

"It's all right."

"No." He held up his hand. "No, I just got so nervous with those cops out front, and then, well ..."

Kennedy just wanted to get his mind off his own embarrassment. After all, she was the one who had brought all this trouble to his doorstep and into his house. "It's ok. What do you have a gun for, anyway?"

He shifted his weight. "That? Oh, well, it's a long story, actually. It looks more like ..."

The door leading to the garage burst open, and two

policemen barged in, weapons raised. Kennedy instinctively raised her hands above her head. Carl let his gun clatter to the floor and did the same.

"Everything's ok, officers." Carl's face was nearly the shade of his Honda in the light from one of the men's flashlights.

"It was just a mistake," Kennedy hastened to explain. "I came out to look for some Tylenol, and, um, I think I startled everyone. I'm sorry."

The men looked tense but lowered their weapons.

"You got a permit for that?" the older one asked Carl.

He let out a little chuckle. "Actually, I was just going to tell Kennedy …"

"Carl? Is that you?" Sandy came bustling in, tying her bathrobe sash around her waist. Her brown hair was in a long French braid that wound around and fell over one shoulder. "Is everything all right out here?" She stopped when she saw the officers standing near the door.

"Looks like everything's just fine, ma'am."

"Well, thank you for being diligent." Sandy gave a nod that was far more dignified than Kennedy could have offered if she had been the one in fluffy pink slippers.

The older policeman nudged his partner. "Well, if that's all …" He let his voice trail off and tipped the brim of his hat.

"Oh, nonsense." Sandy bustled into the kitchen, threw on the lights, and opened the fridge. "Since you're already inside, you better grab a few cinnamon rolls. It'll only take a minute or two to heat them up."

The men looked at each other.

"You've had a long night," Sandy reminded them.

"You go wait back outside. I'll be out in a few," the older one said.

"I'll send extra rolls out with him when they're ready." The young man had already shut the door to the garage behind him when Sandy shouted, "Do you want some coffee, too? I have cream and sugar."

The middle-aged officer hooked his fingers in his belt loop and leaned forward on his toes. "Well, since I'm here, mind if I have a look around?"

"Go right ahead," Sandy answered with her face in the fridge. "The bathroom's down the hall and to the right."

Carl positioned himself in the policeman's way. "Now, wait a minute. Using the pot's one thing, and you're welcome to it. But searching the house, you guys need a warrant for something like that, don't you?"

Sandy stood up. "He's just trying to help us out."

"I know that." Carl gave a nod of respect. "And I'm mighty thankful for that, but it's the principle of the thing, see? Today, we let you come in and walk around for our own safety. Tomorrow ..."

"Tomorrow what?" Sandy interrupted, wiping her hands on the sides of her robe. "Tomorrow they come back to see more pictures of the grandkids?" She nodded at the officer. "Feel free to snoop around as much as you'd like. Makes me feel safer knowing you guys are looking out for us at times like these."

The officer shot a quick glance over to Carl, who nodded his acquiescence. Somehow, just being in the same room as the policemen sent Kennedy's insides quivering like the little bowls of Jell-O that Reuben loved so much.

He sauntered down the hall.

Sandy pecked her husband's cheek. "Sorry, hon, but you know sometimes you just gotta accept the help when it's there."

That was the last either of them said of their disagreement. As the policeman sauntered down the hall, Sandy opened her arms to give Kennedy a big hug. "Sorry if all the fuss woke you up. You must still be exhausted."

"Actually, I think I caused it. I came out here to see if you had any Tylenol or something ..."

Sandy pouted. "Of course, sweetie. I should have thought of that myself. And are you still hungry? We've got cinnamon rolls and more cookies, too." She frowned. "Or can I fix you some real food. Not junk."

Kennedy didn't want to be rude. Right now, she wanted to swallow a few pills that would take the edge off her pain and then go to sleep for the next twenty-four hours.

Sandy opened the fridge again and leaned down. She reached back and pulled out a Tupperware. "Carl forgot his lunch the other day. It's chicken soup." She propped the lid open and took a sniff. "Oh, yeah. That's still good. Want me to heat you up a bowl?"

"I'm fine, really. I just wanted a Tylenol if you have any."

"Why, sure. Carl, you go get that pill bottle. It's in my bathroom cupboard, hon."

A few minutes later, the older policeman left with leftover soup, a whole plateful of cinnamon rolls, and cookies to share with his partner outside. Sandy took the pills from Carl, handed them to Kennedy, and was trying to convince her to sit down for a full meal when the lights flicked off.

"That wind." Sandy reached for Kennedy's hand. "You sit tight. We've got flashlights in the drawer over here. Hold on just a sec."

Kennedy listened to the sounds of Sandy's rummaging

and the wind howling outside. She was thankful she wasn't out on the streets and wondered how many children like the Lindgrens' daughter Blessing were stuck outside on a night like this.

Sandy flicked on a flashlight. "Here we go." She brought another one and set it in front of Kennedy. "Well, I guess maybe this is God's way of telling us it's time for bed. What do you think?"

"That's what I've been saying all along," Carl inserted.

The Lindgrens hugged Kennedy good-night, and she dragged herself down the hall to use the bathroom one last time before bed. Why did this have to happen so close to Christmas? She wondered if Reuben was asleep now and thought about him spending Christmas break alone in his dorm. Maybe she should call him tomorrow. Had she brought her phone charger?

After washing her hands and face one last time, Kennedy made her way back to the guest room. As she passed the Lindgrens' bedroom, her neck tingled at the sound of her name. She slowed down and strained her ears.

"… through so much."

She couldn't hear all of Carl's response, but she made out the words *police* and *detective.*

"I don't think it'll go that far. They were so close to that

Gino guy tonight. They'll find him."

Carl cleared his throat. "Well, if he's still at large, she's not flying to her aunt's tomorrow."

"I know," Sandy answered back. "She'll be disappointed spending Christmas away from family."

"She'll stay here."

"Of course she will, but it won't be the same. From her perspective, I mean."

Kennedy turned to head back to her room. She had to get some sleep.

" ... gotta think about witness protection," Carl added.

Kennedy stopped.

"Don't you think it's a little early for that?"

Her pulse sped up like a rocket blasting off into space.

"... up to the detectives, obviously, but if tonight's any indication, these guys aren't going to stop until they've silenced her. Permanently."

Kennedy's mind was screaming at her to run back to bed before someone caught her eavesdropping, but she was paralyzed, as if Gino were in the house with her, studying her every move. A cat stalking a helpless mouse before it makes its fatal pounce.

For a single, impulsive moment, she imagined throwing open the door to Carl and Sandy's room and flinging herself under the blankets like she had done in her parents' bed in New York after waking up from a nightmare.

Only Sandy and Carl weren't her parents.

And this was no nightmare.

She had to turn around, but she was afraid. Was it Carl's comment about witness protection that got her so spooked?

The police were right outside, she reminded herself. Nothing could happen.

Her stomach twisted in her gut. What if Gino got to the policemen first? What if they were already slouched over in their cars, their leftover soup spilled on their laps, their throats slit like in some gruesome horror flick?

No, this wasn't a movie. This wasn't anything like that. The police were here. Their job was to protect her, and she just had to get back to bed. The Tylenol would kick in soon. Everything would look different in the morning. Sleep and daylight were cures for so many fears and anxieties. She held her breath and turned around. Slowly. As if she'd be invisible to any intruder as long as she didn't make any sudden movements.

The hall was still and lifeless. The dozens of pictures lining the Lindgrens' wall stared at her. She could be back to her room in twenty steps or less. Why was she acting so silly? She was an adult now. She didn't have to live her life in this sort of fear. She was a Christian. She had victory over fear. Over trauma. Over terror.

She put one bare foot in front of the other, feeling guilty and sheepish now for eavesdropping at the Lindgrens' door. Was she a ten-year-old again?

One day, she'd tell Reuben all about it, and they'd laugh. He could tease her about it if he wanted, but instead he'd say something nice and comforting, something to soothe over Kennedy's embarrassment.

She opened the door to the guest room. Never had a bed looked more inviting. Her arm was already starting to feel better. A placebo, maybe? She didn't think Tylenol worked that quickly. It didn't matter. All she needed now was sleep.

She shut the door gently behind her but couldn't relax. Outside, the wind howled. A tree branch scratched the window. Had the police noticed that when they did their rounds? Did they realize how easily someone could climb the tree, enter through the window and ...

No, she couldn't think that way.

The Lord is my shepherd. I shall not be in want.

Wasn't Psalm 23 supposed to make everyone feel warm and fuzzy inside?

She wondered what her mom was doing right now. She sometimes thought about her at the most random times. She stretched out in the bed, wrapping the blankets around herself. The Lindgrens kept their thermostat lower here than at the dorms on campus. Or maybe it just felt colder from the sound of the wind howling outside.

Sandy's story of her daughter had gotten Kennedy thinking about anyone unfortunate enough to be sleeping out on the streets, especially during a windstorm like this. How many teens had she passed this semester in the T station who didn't have anywhere else to go for shelter? All this while Kennedy studied at Harvard, ate three square meals a day and all the snacks she wanted until she was well on her way to earning the notorious freshman fifteen pounds. It wasn't fair. It wasn't right.

If Kennedy had learned one thing about life this past semester, it was that the world was a dangerous, cruel place full of dangerous, cruel people. Kids kidnapped. Girls victimized and abused. Families homeless. Addicts selling themselves on street corners, addicts who had parents who loved them just as much as Carl and Sandy loved Blessing.

There was so much ugliness. People suffering so many different forms of indignity. Besides Carl and Sandy, what was anyone doing about it? What was Kennedy doing about it? Sure, one day she hoped she'd become a doctor, and she'd have plenty of opportunities to help people then. But what about right now? She wasn't lifting a finger to help anyone less fortunate than she was, and the last time she tried she ended up getting kidnapped.

She shut her eyes, trying to block out the noise of the howling wind and her accusing conscience. She couldn't do anything for anybody as exhausted as she was. She would feel better in the morning. She just had to get to sleep.

Why did knowing the power was off make the dark that much more threatening? This was supposed to be her first semester of real independence. How had she grown so afraid?

She had to force her mind and her body to relax. Sandy's story about Blessing and all the hardships the family endured must have gotten Kennedy thinking too hard. Worrying too much. There would always be Blessings. There would always be souls needing to be saved. Kennedy couldn't help them all. And if she didn't focus on herself, taking care of her own body and getting the rest she needed, she wouldn't be able to help anybody.

She took several deep breaths, deliberately relaxing one muscle after another. She was finally warming up underneath the blankets. Everything was all right now. She was cozy. She was cared for. She was safe.

A noise from beneath the bed. Kennedy jostled. This was ridiculous. She wasn't a child anymore. She was sick of being scared. She shut her eyes and focused once more on her breathing.

Slow.

Steady.

She curled underneath the blankets with her back to the window. The wind could howl. The storm could rage. She was relaxed. She would let peace wrap itself around her like an extra layer of warmth. Everything was fine now. Everything was …

"Don't move."

A hand wrapped over her mouth. She squirmed, thrashing her legs, but he leaned over and pinned her down.

"Not a sound."

Kennedy had never heard that voice before. There were no lights in the room to see his face or form. Still, she knew exactly who it was.

Gino.

CHAPTER 23

"Get up."

She obeyed. Something hard pressed up against her back. She should scream. That's all she had to do. Just scream. Scream and alert the Lindgrens. The police would come, and Kennedy would be safe.

Right?

Safe. Was it possible? No. He had a gun. The bullet would pierce her heart or lungs before she finished sounding the alarm, and Gino could dash out the window, climb down the tree, and be off before the police could give him any chase. Maybe they'd catch him, but with all the lights out in the neighborhood and the time it would take them to realize what happened …

Kennedy held her breath.

"That's right." His voice was gruff.

She trembled a little in his grasp, and he tightened his arm around her neck.

"You run, you die."

Kennedy had no trouble believing each word. She nodded to communicate her understanding.

Her self-defense class had taught her some fancy moves to get out of a bear hold. Her instructors never said what to do if the attacker's got a gun pressed up to your back. She was so weak from fear she doubted she could have fought him off even if he had been unarmed.

How had he gotten in? For a moment, answering that one question seemed even more important than escape. How did he manage to get in here while the police were outside watching? There had to be some explanation, right? Otherwise she was dealing with something demonic and supernatural. But that couldn't be. Those kinds of things were only in paranormal novels, which Kennedy avoided as a rule. He had to be human, which meant he had to have entered the house by human means, which meant he wasn't all-powerful.

Which meant that if she was very lucky, she might get out of this alive.

A sudden urge to chuckle welled up from somewhere deep within her belly. She swallowed down the impulse but wondered where it came from. She thought of the campus doctor in his white lab coat scrawling notes about PTSD on his little pad of paper, and somehow it seemed so comical.

You think I had issues back then? You should see what I'm going through now.

The desire to laugh made its way to her chest cavity, bringing a lightness completely foreign to her.

Who needs a psychoanalyst? Just get me some laughing gas.

No. That was fear talking. Hysteria, maybe. Something was trying to take over her brain. It must be some defense mechanism or other, some primitive instinct designed to shield her from the horrors of death. She wondered how evolutionists would explain it. How in the name of natural selection could people evolve to actually laugh in their final moments before their murder? Sure, it might make their death seem less frightening, but it certainly wasn't a trait they could pass on to their offspring from the grave.

Her body was shaking in silent heaves. If she had been brave enough to actually make noise, she wasn't certain if it would sound more like laughter or sobbing.

Gino kept his iron grip around her neck. "We're going to the garage now. No sudden moves. No noise, or I kill you and your friends here. Got it?"

Kennedy nodded. Hadn't she read dozens of scenarios just like this in all the mysteries and thrillers she used to devour in her free time? In not a single one of them had the hero or heroine fallen prey to a laughing fit.

Yet another reason to cross those books off her Christmas reading list.

"Now open that door real slow." His breath was hot on her ear, and her body went rigid. The shaking fit eased up, and for a moment her mind was clear.

He was going to take her to the garage.

And then he was going to murder her.

She didn't think her limbs would respond, and she observed herself with a somewhat detached curiosity as her hand reached for the bedroom doorknob, turning it slightly. She winced, hoping it wouldn't squeak.

"Down the hall." Gino's voice had an almost hypnotic quality, as if Kennedy were a sleep-walker. No, maybe someone already half-dead. Something out of those zombie movies Willow liked. She could carry out simple commands but had no real will. No real volition.

She put one foot in front of the other and could feel Gino's tense body behind her as he pushed her down the dark hall. She prayed Carl and Sandy wouldn't hear. She prayed they wouldn't come out. One false move, one scare, and they might all end up dead.

Was she ready for heaven? No, not really. There was so much more she had expected out of life. Studying with

Reuben. Graduating college. Going on to medical school. Falling in love. Starting a family.

Dizziness seized her, and she reached her hand out to steady herself along the wall. She couldn't see them, but her fingers caressed the frames of so many pictures. Pictures of children and grandchildren. Foster babies. Grandbabies. Each one so precious. Each one so beautiful.

God, I want to live.

She thought about the North Korean refugees her parents took in, Christians with courage to risk their lives to carry the gospel back home. They each expressed their willingness — even their desire — to die doing the work of the Lord.

Kennedy sometimes figured by the time she was old and gray, she might feel the same way.

But not now. Not like this. Would her parents fly her body for burial in Yanji? How would you even transport a corpse overseas?

Her lungs seized up, and she gasped for air. Gino tightened his arm around her neck and pushed her forward.

Her thoughts turned toward Reuben. What would he say? Would he cry?

Reuben.

She had to see him again. She couldn't just die.

They turned the corner to the kitchen. A few more feet, and they'd be in the garage. Her self-defense instructor's voice echoed in her mind. "If he gets you in a car, your chances of survival drop dramatically."

No. She wasn't a statistic. She wasn't a victim. She would survive.

She tucked in her chin, ready to fling her head back. She paused only for a second. He might shoot her right then, but how would dying now be any different than dying in ten minutes or twenty minutes or whenever he took her to her final destination? She thought of the poem *The Highwayman* she had memorized in high school. Bess, the landlord's daughter, fires a rifle that is jammed up against her breast in order to warn her lover, sacrificing her own life to sound the alarm. It had to be now. Either she would surprise him enough to make her escape, or she would die, but at least her death might alert Carl and Sandy and the policemen outside.

Justice would be served.

She sucked in her breath and prepared to give him a head butt he would remember for weeks, even if it was her last act on this earth.

"Not so fast, buddy."

Kennedy's body froze, and her eyes squeezed shut in

the blinding light of a flashlight. Gino rammed the gun even harder into her back. "What do you think you're doing?" he snarled.

Kennedy blinked one eye open to see Carl in the kitchen. In one hand was a flashlight. In the other was a gun pointed right at her.

CHAPTER 24

"How 'bout you put that gun down, boy." Carl's voice was threatening, like the neighbor's pit bull that had terrorized Kennedy when she was growing up.

She was so startled, for a moment she forgot her fear entirely and only wondered if Sandy knew how mean her husband could sound if he really wanted to.

"What're you gonna do if I don't?" Gino crouched to hide most of his body behind Kennedy.

Carl kept his gun poised at them both. "I'll give you one guess."

Gino shifted from one foot to another but stayed planted behind her. "You can't do that. What's gonna stop you from shooting the chick?"

"First of all, she's not a *chick*. She's a young woman, and a very bright and capable one. Second of all, I assume you plan to kill her anyway." He squinted one eye and took aim.

"Yeah, but ..." Gino's voice was infused with an

infective nervousness. "You take me out, you take her out, too."

Carl shrugged. "Probably. But I know her soul is saved. And I seriously doubt yours is. So she dies and goes straight to heaven, and you ... Well, I'd be willing to bet my retirement savings that you wouldn't join her there."

"This is crazy, man."

Kennedy had to agree with Gino's assessment. Something was wrong. This wasn't Carl. This wasn't the pastor she grew up with. What happened to him?

"Crazy or not, you let her go, or you're a dead man, Gino."

"Dude, you're insane."

Carl cocked his head to the side. "Might be. But I won't even need to plead criminal insanity in this case. You're in my house. My house is my castle. And I'll do anything and everything within my power to protect my castle and the people in it."

Kennedy wondered how heroines in her mom's historical fiction novels could faint at the slightest sign of trauma or fear. If she could pass out on cue, she definitely would have by now.

"It's up to you, Gino." Carl talked as smoothly and as easily as if he were practicing for a Sunday sermon.

Kennedy's mind couldn't take in the rest of the words. It was too real to be a dream. Maybe she really had lost her mind. She could hear Carl's voice in her head, could understand the individual words he spoke, but they didn't make any sense when she strung them together.

Maybe he's as insane as I am.

Then she had a thought. What if Carl wasn't really talking to Gino? What if he was talking to her? What if his words contained some secret code? Didn't people do that in spy movies sometimes? Kennedy could swear she saw something like that once with her dad. What was it? Morse code with the eyelids, maybe? She had to focus.

"You see, what Kennedy and I know is that none of us are worthy to go to heaven. We're all sinners. None of us worse than any other, at least in God's eyes."

Was Carl preaching to him now?

Pay attention, she ordered herself. *There has to be something in his words. Some hidden message. Think.*

"And that's why Jesus came, to be the perfect sacrifice, to take away the penalty for all our sins."

No. They were all insane. Carl. Gino. Kennedy. That's all there was to it. They had all gone mad, and somebody was going to die.

"So now's a good time to ask yourself, Gino," Carl

went on, "who do you really serve? Are you willing to bow your knees to the God of the heavens, the one who made the earth and the sky and the sea and all that is in them? Or are you going to keep on worshipping the devil, the father of lies?"

He was inching his way to the side, and for the first time Kennedy guessed what he might be doing. He was distracting Gino, or at least trying to. Maybe he thought Gino wouldn't notice his movements and let him sneak around from the side to get a clearer shot. She stood with her body tense, her ears already ringing in anticipation of gunfire.

"Freeze! Police!"

Kennedy must have closed her eyes because she didn't see anything. She heard the forceful shouts, felt the vibrations of heavy boots on the floor. A scream. Someone plowed into Kennedy, knocking out her breath, tackling her and crashing to the floor.

After that, it was like she was hearing everything from underwater — a strange, high-pitched squeal humming above the muffled noise.

"You have the right to remain silent."

Was that the policeman? He wasn't arresting Carl, was he? He had only been trying to help.

She glanced over to see Gino on the floor while one of the cops cuffed his hands behind his back.

Sandy rushed up and knelt on the floor. Carl was doubled over beside Kennedy, and she realized he had been the one who threw her to the ground.

"He's been hit." Sandy's voice rose higher in pitch with each word. "Someone help. My husband's been shot."

ALANA TERRY

CHAPTER 25

Kennedy had never experienced a tornado, but she imagined it must be like this, only she was in the middle, sitting right in the eye of the storm while the chaos swarmed and spiraled around her. One of the policeman led Gino outside in his cuffs while his partner knelt down by Carl and radioed the ambulance. Kennedy didn't want to look at Carl. Didn't want to face him. The bullet had been meant for her. If something happened to him ...

Sandy put a hand on Kennedy's shoulder. "You okay, hon? You didn't get hurt, did you?"

Kennedy clinched her throat shut and shook her head. No, she hadn't been hit. Only Carl.

Dear God, you can't let him die.

It wasn't fair. How could someone like Carl lie there bleeding on the floor while Gino just walked away in cuffs? Silent sobs shook her body. The world was even more topsy-turvy than she had previously imagined.

Sandy wrapped her up in a warm embrace, but it only

made Kennedy feel even more wretched. She wasn't the one bleeding. She wasn't the one who had taken a bullet to save someone else. What had she done to deserve Sandy's love and comfort?

A hand reached out and grasped hers. It was tough. Calloused.

Pastor Carl.

"I'm sorry," he whispered. "I shouldn't have ..."

Sandy tried to shush him, encouraged him to save his energy, but Carl wouldn't be dissuaded.

"I never meant to scare you. You know I never would've done anything to hurt you." His voice sounded so pained. Kennedy started shaking even more uncontrollably.

"Ambulance will be here in about two minutes." It was the policeman talking. Kennedy tried to hold onto his words, but it sounded like his voice was receding and then rushing ahead at full speed. "Are you going to want to ride with your husband, ma'am?"

Sandy didn't answer.

"You can't leave Kennedy here alone," Carl breathed.

Kennedy wished the earth would just open up its mouth and swallow her up, forever burying her and her mortification. Even as he lay bleeding to death next to her, Carl was still thinking of her comfort, her safety.

Sandy took in a deep breath. "I think Kennedy and I will take the Honda and meet you there at Providence."

The policeman cleared his throat. "Beg your pardon, but the car's taped off right now."

"The car?" Sandy repeated. "Why?"

"We're pretty sure that's how Gino got in the house in the first place. In the trunk."

The trunk? So he had been inside the car while Carl and Kennedy were driving? But when would he have found the time to hide in there? While they were at the hospital, maybe? Kennedy remembered Carl talking to the policeman before he opened up the garage door and parked, safe and secure, locked up in his little castle. Only Gino had been in here the whole night. Just waiting. Just biding his time.

"I can stay here with Kennedy," Sandy suggested.

No. No, they couldn't do that. Carl and Sandy needed to be together. They needed ...

Sirens wailed outside and came to a stop. Their lights flashed through the window. Kennedy forced her eyes to focus on Carl. The top of his back was bloody, but there weren't huge puddles on the floor as she had feared.

"Is he going to be ok?" she whispered faintly as the policeman got up to show the paramedics in.

Sandy kept her arms wrapped around Kennedy shoulders. "Of course, darling."

"What's that you two yakking about over there?" Carl's voice regained some of its usual jocularity.

"Kennedy was just worried about you, that's all. I told her they'd need a whole lot more than a bullet to take my husband down."

"You got that right." Carl's laugh sounded weak, but it still made Kennedy's whole body fill with a delicious warmth. "Nobody better start planning my funeral yet. When my time comes, everyone here's gonna know it, and there's not going to be any doctors or nurses or policeman who are going to try to hold me back, I'm telling you that much. When God opens those gates for me, you bet your life I'll be speeding on my way. I might look back once, but that would just be to say good-bye to my sweetheart."

Carl and Sandy exchanged a glance that was more radiant, more loving, more passionate than any kiss from those romance movies Kennedy's mom liked to watch.

"Let's get out of these folks' way and let them do their work." Sandy helped Kennedy to her feet. "I should have asked you first if you wanted to go with us to the hospital. I just didn't feel right about leaving you here all by yourself after everything. But then again, you're so tired …"

"No," Kennedy interrupted. The idea of staying here alone was nearly paralyzing, but she wasn't about to get in the way of Sandy riding with Carl in the ambulance. Besides, she was exhausted. "No, I don't mind staying here."

Her voice must not have sounded very convincing, because Sandy cocked her head to the side and raised an eyebrow. "We could ask the policemen. They might be able to drop you off at the ER."

Kennedy and Sandy made way for the paramedics, who were getting ready to transfer Carl onto the stretcher.

"That's ok," Kennedy replied. "I'm really tired." She didn't have to make that part up. In fact, once she got to sleep, she'd probably be able to snooze right through the apocalypse.

"Besides," Kennedy added, "I know you probably want to be with Carl. Just to make sure everything ... Just to see that ..."

"What? Him?" Sandy waved her hand in the air. "God knows his work here is far from finished. He's gonna be just fine."

"Amen!" boomed Carl's loud voice from the stretcher. "So what's the plan? You two ladies riding in style with us?"

"Actually ..." began one of the paramedics.

"I know, I know." Carl gave Kennedy a wink. "Immediate family members only."

She really hoped he wasn't going to tell them she was his daughter.

"Kennedy's going to stay here and get some rest," Sandy answered for her. "As long as you're sure she's safe," she added with a nod to the police officer.

"We'll call someone to stay in the house just to cover all our bases."

"I'd appreciate that." Sandy looked down and brushed off her floral nightgown. "I guess I better go get dressed."

A few minutes later, a silence settled into the woodwork and paneling of the Lindgrens' guest room, the eerie, almost ghostly quiet after a storm. If Kennedy had the energy to worry, she might have felt afraid. If she had the mental capacity, she might have stayed up praying for Carl's healing, but the paramedics had seemed so calm. They joked with Carl as they wheeled him out the front door. Sandy followed them wearing a quiet, beautiful peace around her like a shawl. Or maybe a crown.

Kennedy's mind spun in small, lazy spirals, the same sensation she got after staying up way too late with her dad to watch a movie. She couldn't string the whole plot together, but some of the chase scenes and more intense moments floated through her mind, letting her recapture the emotions she experienced even if she couldn't remember the details.

Her body was heavy, but her mind was surprisingly light. Maybe it was the exhaustion. Maybe it was the security that came from knowing her attackers were all in custody and there was an armed officer sitting on the Lindgrens' couch. She shut her eyes and inhaled deeply.

Never before had she been more grateful for a pillow and blankets.

Never before had she been more ready to sleep.

CHAPTER 26

The sun was streaming in through the bedroom window when the doorbell woke Kennedy up the next morning.

Her heart leaped up to her trachea for just a moment as all the memories from the previous night crashed and collided into her thoughts at once. She stood up. Who could it be?

She held her breath as she tiptoed down the hall. There was a different policeman in the living room now, and he stood and nodded at the window. "You know that guy?"

She glanced and saw the painted youth group van parked in the Lindgrens' driveway, the winter sun reflecting off its bright tie-dye swirls. She peeked through the window near the front door. The first thing she saw was the blond dreadlocks.

"Yeah, I know him." She ran her fingers through her hair as the officer fidgeted with the deadbolt on the Lindgrens' front door.

"Nick!" She smiled at the St. Margaret's youth pastor,

trying to remember how long it had been since the last time she saw him.

"Sandy called me. Said you might want a ride over to Providence." His hair reached nearly down to his waist. It was always a temptation for Kennedy to reach out and give it a good, strong tug. "I tried calling your cell, but it kept going right to voicemail."

"Yeah, that's the dumb battery. Sorry about that."

Nick turned his head from one side to the other to stretch. "Hey, it's no problem. I was gonna stop and see if they needed anything anyway. It's not even out of my way to swing by here first. I can take you now, or wait in the van if you need time to get ready."

Kennedy had slept in her clothes. Her bag was in Carl's car, but she wasn't sure if the police still had everything roped off.

"I just need to use the bathroom. What time is it?"

Nick stuck his hands in his pockets. "Almost one. Did I wake you up?"

It must have been pretty obvious by the way she looked.

"Hey, don't worry," Nick added. "I would have slept in, too. Sounds like you had a crazy night."

"Something like that. If you don't mind waiting, I can

be out in just a minute or two."

He jingled the keys in his hand. They were attached to a lanyard with patterns of Jesus fish and surfboards in all the colors of the rainbow. "Sure thing. I'll be in the van. I just got a new Christmas album, so take your time."

"If you're headed out, I'll check everything one last time and be on my way," the policeman replied.

Kennedy thanked him and headed to the bathroom. A few minutes later, she was in the old VW bus with Nick, headed toward the hospital. "How's Carl doing?" Kennedy was almost too afraid to ask, but the uncertainty would have eventually erupted into hundreds of worry pimples all over her body if she didn't find out soon. Had he made it through the night ok? Had he lost too much blood?

"From what Sandy said on the phone, sounds like he's doing great. You know Carl. Already invited one of the nurses to Christmas Eve service. Got another one interested in doing ultrasounds once the new pregnancy center ever gets its own machine."

Kennedy's shoulders relaxed. So he couldn't be that bad.

"What about you?" Nick asked. "You holding up all right?"

Kennedy hadn't bothered to ask herself that question

yet today. She knew it would take a while to process everything she had gone through. Logically, it all sounded like great news, all except for the part about Carl getting shot and his car so banged up. But Vinny and Gino were both behind bars, and as far as she knew, there was no one else around who had any reason to harm her.

"I'm just glad it's finally over."

It was over, wasn't it? She already felt more relaxed than she had in weeks. How long had it been since she slept in so late?

Nick strummed the steering wheel as if he were playing an imaginary guitar along with his acoustic Christmas CD. Kennedy had never heard of the band, but she liked the simple, folksy sound. The bobble-head set of Peter, James, and John on the dashboard jiggled when he slowed down to turn toward Providence.

"What about ... I don't know ... all the stuff you went through earlier? Was it hard for you yesterday, reliving that all over again?"

The unseen fist that had taken residence in her gut for the past half a semester seized her insides and wrenched them in its iron grasp. So much for that sense of tranquility.

"It wasn't easy." She forced a little laugh that was far too high pitched for her vocal range. "Just pray you never have to face Carl while he's waving around a gun."

Nick slowed to a stop at a red light. "What?"

Kennedy told him how Carl had been in the kitchen, blocking the way before Gino could get her into the garage.

"He's really still got that thing?" Nick asked. "After all these years?"

"What thing?" Kennedy stared at the van's paint job through the side mirror. The kaleidoscope of colors almost made her dizzy. On her door was a scene of Moses parting a sea full of tropical fish, with surfing flamingos riding the waves.

"Oh, he never told you the story behind that gun?" Nick turned down the music. "Well, he and Sandy had their share of issues when they first got married. Stupid people would give them a hard time — bunch of racist bigots, really."

Kennedy nodded.

"Well, it got so bad in one instance, Carl got himself a license and a gun and took a firearms safety class."

"I never realized it got that bad," Kennedy admitted, trying to figure out who could have made the Lindgrens feel so unsafe Carl would have resorted to such measures.

"I know, right?" Nick asked. "I mean, when he tells these stories, it's like I'm living back in the dark ages. But they were in the south back then. And you know Carl. He'd do just about anything to protect his family."

Kennedy thought about last night, how he had dived at her to get her out of the way. How would she have felt if he really had died for her? How could she ever have looked Sandy in the eye again?

"Well, so he had this gun, and as time went on people became more and more accepting of others, so he never really needed it. Then one winter — I think it was my first Christmas at St. Margaret's — someone breaks in to the Lindgrens' home. Just a kid, really. Seventeen or eighteen, I don't remember all the details, but not a hardened crook or anything. He was just looking for a few quick things he could sell for easy money around Christmastime. I don't think he realized the Lindgrens were home. Probably thought they were on vacation or something. Anyway, Carl hears the noise in the living room, comes out with his gun, and sees this kid poking around under the Christmas tree. And the boy stands up and recognizes Carl and says, 'Aren't you that guy from that big church off the Red Line? My grandma makes me go there every Christmas.' So of course Carl puts the gun away, and then he and Sandy sit him down and he ends up accepting Christ, they invite him and his mom and his grandma over for Christmas dinner, and it's all one big happy ending. But after that, at least as Carl explains it, he decided he just couldn't be a pastor and keep a gun at the same time. He got rid of all the ammo, but he joked about holding onto the pistol just for show if he ever needed to scare someone away. I guess he was serious, though, if he still had it last night."

Kennedy was trembling again. Would she ever be able to talk about the things she had gone through without her muscles all spasming at once? It made more sense now, at least logically, how Carl could have stood there with his gun pointed at her. Part of her had known the whole time he was bluffing, but that wasn't enough to stop her insides from quivering with the memories.

"What about you?" Nick asked as he pulled the van into the Providence parking garage. "You have big plans for Christmas or anything?"

Kennedy hadn't thought that far ahead but was glad to change the subject and talk about something more mundane. "I'm supposed to fly to Baltimore to visit my aunt for a few weeks, but now I'm not sure what's going on."

She'd have to get her phone charged and get in touch with Aunt Lilian. Her parents, too. And she could only guess how many phone calls she had missed from

Detective Drisklay by now. With so many meetings and deadlines and demands on her time, it almost felt as if she was still in the middle of her semester at Harvard.

The chances of her getting to the airport in time for her four o'clock flight today were pretty slim. She didn't want to leave until she was convinced Carl was better, and she had enough experience with the police department to know she'd have to answer a lot of questions over the next few days. Maybe she would stay at the Lindgrens' and help take care of Carl while he healed. There had to be some way to repay him for his courage.

Nick maneuvered the VW bus in between a flower delivery van and a pickup. Peter, James, and John kept bobbling even after he parked.

"You ready?"

She nodded. Twenty-four hours ago, she had been preparing to take her last final of the semester. Now she was about to go visit the man who had saved her life from a dangerous criminal. Out of the dozens or maybe even hundreds of thrillers she had read over the years, none of them had prepared her for the relief, the almost euphoric release that came from knowing her captors were in custody. But the joy was tarnished, polluted by the guilt that had glared her in the face ever since she saw Carl's bloody shirt. That bullet had been meant for her. How could she be happy, how could she be relieved when her pastor was in the hospital recovering from a bullet wound — a bullet wound he would have never suffered if it hadn't been for her?

"You ok?" Nick asked. "You look pretty serious."

Kennedy forced a smile. "I'm fine." She followed him toward the hospital entrance, each of her footsteps shouting hostile accusations in her ear.

The wind from last night had died down, and the sky was gray and overcast.

"I'm glad you were able to come with me." Nick let Kennedy go first through the hospital entrance.

Providence's interior was decorated with blue and silver tinsel, with large red Christmas ornaments hanging from the ceiling.

He unbuttoned his coat. "I'm sure Carl and Sandy will be excited to see you."

Kennedy wasn't that certain, but she kept the thought to herself.

CHAPTER 27

"Nick! Kennedy!" Sandy rushed toward them with open arms. After hugging Kennedy, she turned to Nick and put both hands on his shoulders. "What's the deal with this shirt? You relearning your ABCs?"

Nick grinned and pointed to the two sets of alphabets. "The first one's missing the L. Get it? The first ... *No el.* Like the carol."

Sandy rolled her eyes and tucked her arm around Kennedy's waist. "Well, at least you guys are here. Carl's been worrying about you."

"I have not," came the gruff voice from the hospital bed.

Kennedy was used to seeing Carl in button-down shirts and slacks. She was almost embarrassed to witness him lying there in the blue and white floral hospital gown.

"Come on, I don't look that bad, do I?" He stretched one arm out to give Kennedy a hug and turned to Nick. "Gonna shake you left-handed today, if you don't mind."

"How you doing, Pastor Carl?"

It was weird to hear Nick call him *Pastor*, but Kennedy couldn't figure out why. Maybe because Nick was older than she was, and she had dropped the *pastor* title almost immediately after reconnecting with him here in the States.

"I'm all right." Carl's voice was strong. Booming. That in itself sent waves of relief coursing through her veins. "Doctor said I've got a fractured shoulder blade, but I'm just thankful to be alive and kicking."

"Daddy?"

Kennedy didn't recognize the woman standing in the doorway. Her heels made her look at least three inches taller than she really was. She rushed past Kennedy and Nick to Carl's bedside.

"I got Mom's text this morning, but I'm out of sick days, so I had to wait for my lunch break." She glanced at the clock on the wall. "The T took forever. I've only got ten minutes before I have to head back."

"You didn't have to come all this way, sweetie." Sandy gave the woman a loving pat on the back. "You could have just called to talk to him."

She sniffed. "I wanted to come by in person. Make sure … You know, make sure …"

"Your old man's not about to croak?" Carl laughed. "Not

anytime soon, babe. You're just gonna have to wait three or four more decades to get that massive inheritance check."

"Dad!" Her tone made her sound like an exasperated teenager.

Sandy took a deep breath. "Well, sweetie, now you're here. You can see your father's fine." She smiled at Kennedy and Nick. "This is our daughter, Blessing. And you remember our youth pastor, right?"

Blessing gave a little smirk and crossed her arms. "Yeah, I remember you."

Nick replied with something of a half-smile of his own and didn't say anything.

"And this," Sandy went on, "is the Sterns' daughter. You remember Roger and Juliette Stern from the church back in the city?"

"No." Blessing shrugged at Kennedy. "But I remember hearing all about you on the news."

"Well now," Sandy inserted before her daughter could say anything else, "where's Tyson today?"

"With his other grandma." Blessing glanced again at the clock above Carl's head.

Sandy frowned. "I'm sorry I couldn't watch him."

"Of course you can't. You're here with Daddy, right where you're supposed to be."

"And she won't leave me alone," Carl complained. "Keeps threatening to beat up the nurses who come in here to take care of me." He winked.

Kennedy glanced at Nick, who looked about as out of place as she felt.

"You gonna be home by Christmas?" Blessing asked.

Carl adjusted his bed so he was sitting up a little more. "You kidding me? I'm not settling for hospital food when I can have your mother's cooking."

Sandy smiled and patted his hand. "We're hoping so, at least. Doctor says they may have to do surgery."

"Pshaw." Carl waved his left hand in the air. "They're just trying to get more insurance money out of us. That's the way these bureaucracies work. Money, money, money." He fixed his eyes on his daughter. "So the answer to your question, sweetie, is yes, I'll be home for Christmas. You're coming over for dinner, right? You and Tyson and … oh, why do I keep forgetting his name? That guy … one with all the hieroglyphs tatted on his arms …"

Blessing did not look amused. "It's calligraphy."

Carl frowned. "Really? I could have sworn I saw something just like it in the National Geographic special on mummies. Oh, well. Is old what's-his-name coming with you for Christmas?"

"Damion, Dad. His name's Damion."

Carl kept a good-natured tone in spite of the way his daughter glared at him. "That's the one. Keep wanting to call him Dalmatian for some reason. *Here, boy. Here Dalmatian.*"

Sandy put her hand on Blessing's shoulder. "What your father means is we'd love to have you over for Christmas dinner, of course. All *three* of you." She shot Carl a look laced with warning.

"That's right." He nodded. "All three of you."

"Good." Sandy frowned at the clock and turned to Blessing. "Now you should get yourself back to work so you don't get in trouble with your supervisor, and I'll call you to let you know if I can watch Tyson on Friday."

"All right." Blessing gave her dad a quick peck on the cheek before heading out.

Kennedy watched the way Nick's whole body relaxed when she left. Sandy let out a loud sigh. "Well, Kennedy, did you sleep all right last night?"

Kennedy felt guilty when she admitted that she had. "What about you?" she added. "Did either of you get to sleep?"

Sandy smiled. "Oh, Carl was knocked out like a baby. Whatever they pumped through that IV must've been some miracle maker. I haven't seen him sleep that soundly in ten years or more."

Carl snorted. "I told you we should have gone to Hawaii last summer, didn't I? Didn't I say we were due for a vacation?"

Sandy smiled but didn't respond.

"So we can't afford three thousand dollars for a week in Hawaii, so we'll spend our five thousand dollar deductible instead for a staycation at Providence. Food's not as good, but boy, do you sleep like a rock."

"Well, one of us does." The corners of Sandy's eyes wrinkled up when she spoke. "I was lucky to get that half hour snooze between the x-rays and the doctor consult. They wanted him to have surgery last night," she explained to Kennedy and Nick. "Make sure everything looked all right. But he said …"

Carl waved his good hand in the air. "I said of course it wouldn't look all right if they went in there with a scalpel and started moving things around that have no business moving."

Sandy shrugged her shoulders. "So the doctor decided we could wait a few days and see."

"I still don't know what all the fuss is about," Carl insisted. "I feel fine as long as they keep that IV bag filled.

I'm not dead. My ticker's as healthy as a teenager's — doctor said so himself. But the longer they keep me here, the more they can rack up the medical bills. Probably give all themselves a nice Christmas bonus, too." He reached for his wife's hand. "Remind me, hon, to wait until summer or spring next time I jump in front of a bullet, will ya?"

Sandy cast a furtive glance at Kennedy, who tried to maintain a neutral expression. "Well, sweetie." Sandy's voice sounded far too chipper for the moment. "Have you called your parents or your mom's sister in Maryland?"

Kennedy was a little ashamed to admit she had slept all the way until Nick came knocking at the door, especially after hearing how Sandy had passed her night by Carl's side.

Sandy frowned at the clock. "I guess if Nick was willing to drive, you could make it to the airport in time to catch that flight."

"Absolutely out of the question," someone interrupted from the doorway. Kennedy knew she disliked the voice even before she turned to see who was there behind her.

Detective Drisklay.

He frowned. "You, young lady, have a very bad habit of leaving your phone off when people need to get in touch with you." He had his notebook in one hand, his Styrofoam cup of black coffee in the other. "But since you're all here, we may as well get comfortable." He swept past Nick and sat down on a swivel stool. "All right. Who's gonna start and tell me what happened?"

CHAPTER 28

It was nearly dinnertime before Detective Drisklay was done grilling Kennedy and the Lindgrens. Nick excused himself shortly after the interview started, but Sandy made him promise to take Kennedy home for the evening when everything was done. Sometimes Sandy's sense of protectiveness was smothering, but tonight Kennedy was glad to stay far away from the subway stations.

"So I guess you're not gonna make the flight to your aunt's, huh?" Nick asked as they pulled out of the Providence parking garage that evening.

"No. The detective said I shouldn't go anywhere for a few weeks. There's gonna be tons of questions. Legal stuff. I guess I'm supposed to talk with someone from the district attorney's office tomorrow." She sighed. Being the victim of a high-profile crime was about as time-consuming as her pre-med studies.

"You hungry?"

Kennedy looked at the clock and tried to remember

what she had eaten that day. Just a cold sandwich and fruit salad from the hospital cafeteria. "A little."

"Yeah? 'Cause if you are, I could take you out." Nick's dreadlocks whipped across his face as he turned to look at her and then straightened out to focus again on the road. "I mean, not *out* out, just, you know. Food."

Kennedy was exhausted, but she had to eat something before calling it a night. "Food is good."

Twenty minutes later, they were sitting at a booth in Harvard Square eating soup out of sourdough bread bowls.

"I have to admit, clam chowder is something Boston does way better than New York."

"Oh, yeah?" Nick wiped his face with his napkin. "Because I was just thinking it doesn't quite measure up to Seattle's."

"Are you from Washington?" Kennedy asked.

"Oregon, actually, but I spent a lot of time up and down the West Coast. That was back in my quasi-homeless, semi-nomadic, living-out-of-my-van days."

She raised her eyebrows. "Sounds … interesting."

He stared past her shoulder. "It was magical."

Something about hearing an adult with dread-locks down to his waist using words like *magical* made Kennedy chuckle. "I'll take your word for it."

"Guess they don't have much surfing in China, do they?"

"Not where we were," she answered.

"Yeah, it's no good here, either, but I knew that when I moved. Just one of the costs of discipleship, right?"

She couldn't tell if he was serious or not. "Why did you end up coming out here?"

"Short answer is God got a hold of me. I was always pretty churchy, but that was just one little part of my life, you know? Like, I took math in high school because that's what my guidance counselor told me I had to do to graduate. It didn't mean anything to me outside the classroom walls. That's kinda how church was to me. After college, I sort of burned out on school. My sister, well she had been going through a lot, too. Pretty taxing stuff. So I decided to take a year or two and just see what was real. Got a beat-up van, but it took me down all the way from the Oregon coast to San Diego, then all the way back up to Seattle before I finally came back home."

He dipped a piece of sourdough into his chowder and went on talking with his mouth full.

"Well, something out there just changed me. The ocean. The waves. I don't know. God talks to everyone in different ways, right? Sometimes he uses angels, sometimes he uses a donkey. For me, it was the coast. And I knew I wanted to spend my life helping others. Kids like me, kids who were pretty decent people but who didn't really know Jesus.

"My friend was working at a home for troubled teens out in Vermont. Asked me to join on a Friday. By Sunday after church, I was on the road in my clunker. It got me just over the Rockies before dying. I stuck around there for a couple weeks, volunteered for a few churches, met some great people, and they helped me get fixed up and back on my way."

Nick took a sip of his veggie juice before continuing. "So I worked at the boys home for a few years, then I met Carl. St. Margaret's was growing faster than anyone could have guessed, and he needed help with the youth and children's ministry there, so I settled down and became a Cambridge boy."

Kennedy was trying to guess Nick's age when he asked, "What about you?"

The question caught her off guard. "Me what?"

He adjusted one of his dreadlocks that had fallen in front of his eye. "I don't know. What makes you tick? Why Harvard? Why pre-med?"

Kennedy wasn't sure where to begin. She fidgeted with a piece of sourdough. "Well, I guess I like helping people.

And Harvard had their early-admissions program, so I sort of applied on a whim, and when I got in, well ... It's one of those offers you don't really turn down."

Nick didn't say anything right away, which gave Kennedy plenty of time to think of how ignorant her answer had sounded.

"I've thought a little about medical missions." Why had she added that part? Did she just want to sound more mature? Was she trying to prove that she was ministry-minded like he was?

"These bread bowls are delicious."

Kennedy nodded, grateful Nick was changing the subject.

A few minutes later, he scooted back his chair. "Hey, thanks for joining me. That was a lot of fun." He glanced at the time. "I still have twenty minutes in the parking meter. I could drive you back to Carl and Sandy's now, or we could go for a little walk."

There was something endearing and almost awkward in his expression. Was he asking her out? Or was he just being nice? A year ago, even a month ago, she probably would have been flattered. She glanced outside. The night was already dark. The howling of wind echoed in her memory. What was wrong with her? Wasn't college supposed to be all about living in the moment, being spontaneous, enjoying new people, gaining new experiences? And she didn't want to spend an extra twenty minutes with Nick because the dark made her nervous?

Or was there more to it than that? Reuben's face flitted through her mind, the kind expression in his eyes as he looked at her with so much concern.

Nick frowned. "You know what? I forgot how tired you must be. What do you say we just head back to the van and I'll take you to the Lindgrens' now. We're not too far."

Kennedy tried to sigh away the heaviness in her chest. "No, it's not that, it's just ..." She stopped short. "It's just, I've got a friend back on campus, and I really want to call and let them know I'm safe."

"They're probably pretty worried, right?" Nick's voice was gentle. Subdued.

"Yeah." Kennedy sighed, glad Nick had picked up on her use of the gender-neutral pronoun. "Yeah, if you don't mind, I think I'm ready to head home."

CHAPTER 29

"Thanks so much for dinner." Kennedy couldn't articulate why she felt like apologizing to Nick during the ride back to Carl and Sandy's. "It was great."

Nick pulled the bus into the Lindgrens' driveway. "They make good chowder there, don't they?" For a minute, he looked like he was about to get out of the car too, but then he just gave a little wave. "Well, I'll see you around, I'm sure."

She opened the passenger door. "Yeah. Sandy said you're coming over for dinner Christmas Eve."

He smiled. "I'll be there."

"All right. Thanks again." She failed to infuse as much enthusiasm into her voice as she had intended, but she hoped she at least didn't sound rude.

"Have a good night."

"You, too."

She walked up to the Lindgrens' porch, aware of his eyes following her. It wasn't until her hand was on the knob that she realized she didn't have a key or any way to get in. She was about to wave Nick down to ask to borrow his phone when the door opened.

"Well, there you are!"

Kennedy was so relieved to see Sandy in the doorway she didn't mind the exaggerated wink. "I was *wondering* where you two went. I left Providence at least half an hour after you did." She leaned forward and waved to Nick, who was pulling the bus out of the driveway. "So you got something to eat, did you?" Sandy wrapped an arm around Kennedy's waist and pulled her in. "That was awful thoughtful of Nick. I knew he had it in him to be a romantic when the right woman caught his eye."

"We were both hungry, that's all. It's been a long day."

Sandy insisted on making Kennedy some tea, and once or twice she gave Kennedy a sly smile while she bustled around the kitchen, but she graciously didn't say anything else about Nick.

"The doctor says now Carl might be home by Saturday." Sandy sat down at the table across from Kennedy. "You know that's Carl's first thought. He hasn't missed a Sunday preaching in years."

"That's good." Kennedy's mind was elsewhere, on getting in touch with Reuben, on the Christmas she wasn't going to spend with her parents or her aunt, on the dozens of meetings and legal proceedings ahead of her. She wished she could dump all her memories onto someone else who would testify as her proxy.

"Oh, I almost forgot to tell you. That newspaper reporter stopped by the hospital looking for you." Sandy spoke as casually as if she had been mentioning a missed phone call from the friend next door. "You know which one I mean? The red-haired boy?"

Kennedy had been forced to deal with all kinds of nameless members of the press over the past few months, but one face stuck out in her memory. "Yeah, I know who you're talking about."

"Nice kid." Sandy looked at Kennedy out the corner of her eyes. "Of course, I don't know if he's a Christian like Nick. Do you?"

Kennedy buried her face in her teacup and didn't respond.

"Well, Carl insisted I spent tonight here at home and try to get some rest." Sandy lowered her voice. "Between you and me, I think he just wants the room to himself so he can watch those silly Westerns he likes so much."

"I'm probably going to go to bed soon, too." Kennedy had emailed her aunt, who had probably called her mom, who had probably left fifteen or more voicemails by now. She needed to remember to plug her phone in tonight. She almost envied Carl. People in hospitals could choose not to return phone calls and blame it on the meds or the nurses or any number of convenient excuses.

Kennedy helped Sandy clean the table, tried twice to help with the dishes, and was finally shoved off to bed with a hug and a good-night prayer that left her feeling like she was five years old again. Kennedy fell asleep right away, thoughts of final exams and detective interviews, car chases and failed assassination attempts retreating before the heaviness and exhaustion that had clung to her the whole semester.

CHAPTER 30

The next few days were a blur of meetings. With all those detectives, lawyers, and media gurus vying for her attention, Kennedy wished she could hire a personal assistant just to juggle her schedule.

Sandy was even busier gophering Carl's books and effects to and from his room in Providence. He still insisted on preparing for his Sunday sermon. The doctors weren't giving him a firm release date yet, but the chances of surgery decreased each day.

When he was finally let out Saturday evening, Kennedy rode with Sandy to bring him back home.

"I told you they wouldn't keep me from the pulpit." Carl had lost a few pounds at Providence. His chipmunk cheeks weren't quite as full when he smiled, and he seemed to boast a few more wrinkles than Kennedy remembered. Still, besides having his arm in a sling, he walked and talked and acted like the boisterous, bustling pastor she had known as a little girl in Manhattan.

Sandy stopped by the store on the way home from Providence to pick up Carl's prescription. "I'll just be a minute or two."

"Don't listen to a word she says," Carl whispered when she left. "She'll be in there half an hour if she's in there a second."

Sure enough, when Sandy got back to the car, she was pushing a cart full of grocery bags and several rolls of wrapping paper.

"Sorry it took me so long."

"What were you doing in there?" Carl asked after she had loaded the trunk. "Making plans to feed an army?"

Sandy turned the key in the ignition. "They had ham on sale."

"So you got a whole cart full?"

"No. But I had to get sides to go with it."

Kennedy loved the way Carl and Sandy always bantered back and forth. Her parents had never really been playful like that, at least not in Kennedy's memory.

"Well, it's just Kennedy staying with us. I don't think you needed to break the bank. The skinny thing eats like a bird."

Sandy waved away his remark. "It's for Christmas Eve, silly."

"You know Christmas is a week and a half away, right?" Carl asked.

She pulled out of the parking lot and patted her husband's leg. "You got to plan these things ahead, you know."

Over the next few days, Kennedy grew to understand exactly what kind of planning ahead was required for a Lindgren-style Christmas Eve dinner. She and Sandy started by making ten dozen cookies to serve the grandkids when they came to help decorate the tree. It took a day and a half to reclaim the house and vacuum up all the colored tinsel, cookie crumbs, and popcorn kernels they left behind.

When Christmas week came, Sandy and Kennedy were in the kitchen for at least six hours a day, slicing, cubing, mixing, and chopping. On the days when Sandy babysat her grandson, Kennedy stayed busy with meal prep even while Sandy helped Tyson make his mom, dad, and paternal grandmother hand-made gifts. From looking inside the fridge, you would have assumed their guest count was in the twenties or thirties, and maybe it was. Sandy was extending new invitations and modifying the guest list at least once or twice a day. She had insisted that Kennedy invite Reuben when she learned he had no other place to go, and Kennedy was happy when he accepted.

On the morning of the 24th, Sandy sent Carl out twice to the store for items she forgot but was convinced no Christmas dinner spread could exist without. She and Kennedy had already scrubbed the house spotless over the past few days, but she went over everything two or three more times in the final hours before the guests arrived. Kennedy was glad to know she'd be one of many seated around the Lindgrens' dinner table. She would have hated the thought of Sandy going through so much trouble just for her. She was a little anxious that Reuben would feel out of place, but then she remembered his hundred cousins, aunts, and uncles, and figured he'd probably be more at home than she was.

Carl had spent the past week and a half alternately teasing Sandy for her perfectionistic tendencies and trying in vain to convince her to rest or relax. Tonight, he placed his left hand on her shoulder, smiled into her work-flushed face, and declared, "Everything looks perfect, dear." He kissed her cheek. "You work harder than any other woman I know."

She paused long enough to give him a small peck on the lips and then scurried to the freezer.

"What are you doing?" Carl asked.

"I need to make sure we have enough ice."

"Leave it."

"I just want to …"

"Leave it."

Sandy turned and gave Carl a small, tired smile. He came up and gave her a slow hug. "I love you, babe," he whispered, and Kennedy wondered if they even remembered she was there.

"I love you, too." Sandy nuzzled her cheek against his. "And you know what I could use a strong, hunky man for right about now?"

"What's that?" A playful smirk spread across his face, and Kennedy wondered if she should retreat to the guest room.

Sandy returned his smoldering grin. "You could reach up and pull that extra pack of napkins down for me."

Carl took her hand and kissed it. "Anything for my princess."

The doorbell rang.

"Oh! They're here!" Sandy sounded as excited as a little girl on Christmas morning. "I'll get that," she told Kennedy. "You just sit down and make yourself comfortable."

It would probably be a late night, and a loud one too, judging by the laughter of the two grandsons who burst through the dining room waving toy airplanes through the air and occasionally crashing them into each other.

A third boy ran in to join the ruckus, and Kennedy recognized Blessing's son, Tyson.

A few minutes later, another round of greetings heralded the arrival of more guests. By the end of the night, Kennedy would be lucky to remember half of their names. The sounds were so different from the typical Harvard din. Had she really only been in college for one semester? She was an entirely different person with what felt like a lifetime of experiences — experiences that strengthened and sharpened her, as well as some that left ugly, gaping scars.

"Kennedy!" Sandy's voice was playful and teasing. "There's someone here to see you."

Kennedy jumped up, chiding herself for feeling so nervous. It was just Reuben. It's not like they hadn't seen each other every day in class all semester long.

"Hey." There was his same smile, his same care-free demeanor.

"Hey." She was surprised when he wrapped his arms around her for a hug.

"I'm glad you're safe." He was still wearing his parka, the same one he loaned her during their ride on the T.

She gave Reuben a smile and led him to the appetizer table. Nick was in the corner and gave a quick nod. Kennedy tried not to feel embarrassed. She hadn't done anything wrong.

The Lindgrens' house was a blaze of jumbled colors. Christmas decorations hung on nearly every square foot of wall without any common theme other than cheer. Many of them were homemade and looked like they had survived a few decades in and out of storage boxes. It was all so different from what Kennedy remembered of childhood holidays at her grandma's in New York, where she was the only child amongst somber, formal faces.

It was hard to imagine how recently she and Carl had been driving for their lives, ducking while bullets shattered the window of his car. She would probably still worry when she was out at night. She probably couldn't ride the T for a while without a bad case of the shakes. She'd definitely have her fair share of nightmares with Gino's hardened face glaring at her. But for right now, she could focus on the sound of Carl and Sandy bantering playfully while wave after wave of grandkids took over the dining room, living room, and den. She could forget the smell of subway smoke and burned tire rubber and antiseptic hospitals and fix her mind on the scent of savory ham and fresh coffee.

For now, with the happy shouts and greetings quickly drowning out the sound of the Christmas carols on the stereo, Kennedy could finally relax. She and Reuben sat down with their plates full of candies, veggies, quiches, and mini-sandwiches. Reuben took a bite before announcing, "I got you something for Christmas." He reached into his pocket and pulled out a small box.

She laughed as soon as she opened the present. "You know me too well." It was a new cellphone battery. She hoped it hadn't cost too much money.

"So you'll always have a back-up," Reuben declared with a smile.

"Well, I have something for you, too." She put her plate down and ran to the guest room. She came back with an envelope. "It's not ... I mean, I had a hard time ... Well, just open it."

Reuben tore open the envelope and pulled out the two gift cards. "Common Treasures and Angelo's Pizza?"

"It's the rain check I promised you."

He slipped the cards into his coat. "Thank you."

Sandy bustled over. "Have you two eaten yet? There's lots, so help yourselves."

Kennedy and Reuben looked at their full plates and broke into giggles. Kennedy took a deep breath, thankful

ALANA TERRY

that the Lindgrens had opened their home to her once more, thankful that God had kept her safe through yet another fiery ordeal.

CHAPTER 31

If Carl had teased Kennedy for her small appetite before, he'd have no excuse to do so in the future after seeing how much Christmas dinner she packed away. Only halfway into the main course, she already regretted wearing her tight black skirt. Now she understood Sandy's preference for loose-fitting dresses that didn't hug you anywhere around the waist.

Sandy had pulled out three tables, and even then there were a few guests sitting on the couches eating off TV trays. The overfull, bursting feeling Kennedy felt in her gut grew in proportion to the pressure building up in her brain from all the noise. She couldn't remember the last time she had been around so many children. Had she ever? She and Reuben remained in the corner, laughing about Professor Adell and her atrocious penmanship, giving their best impressions of their calculus TA's Korean accent. They already had plans to check out the bookstore and grab some pizza the day after Christmas.

In the middle of the meal, Carl stood up and clinked his cider glass with his knife. His arm was still in a sling, but he was dressed handsomely in a forest green suit with a striking red tie Sandy had adjusted for him two or three times over the course of the evening.

"Can I have your attention?" His booming voice carried over the dozens of smaller conversations, but it still took half a minute before he could continue.

"Two weeks ago, God took something that could have been tragedy. He took something that I know for a fact the devil would have loved to use for evil, and he brought about good. *What good?* you might be wondering." He raised his glass toward Kennedy. "All those who might have reason to harm our friend here are being brought to justice." He nodded to Blessing. "Our family's closer than ever before." He gave his wife a charming smile. "And I've been reminded every day of my recovery how lucky and blessed I am to have this amazing woman by my side. You mean more than the world to me, babe, and I don't say that lightly."

He kissed the top of Sandy's head, and everyone raised their glasses.

"To the one who does immeasurably more than all we ask or imagine."

Kennedy hadn't heard many toasts before, but this felt more real and more genuine than anything she could have put into words even if she had weeks to prepare. Everyone drank, and several of the grandkids splashed sparkling cider on the kiddie table when they tried to clink their plastic cups together.

"And now I have something to say, too." Blessing's boyfriend stood up. Kennedy hadn't met him officially, but she knew who he was from the way Blessing had draped herself over his lap all evening.

Carl's eyes widened, but he made a broad gesture and sat down. "All right. Here's Dominic now, apparently with something to say to us all this Christmas Eve."

"Damion," Sandy whispered. "His name is Damion."

"Sorry. Go on, Damion."

Kennedy couldn't tell if that was sarcasm creeping into Carl's tone, but she did catch the way he didn't look right at his daughter's boyfriend but instead stared past his shoulder.

Damion took a deep breath and took Blessing's hand.

"I'm not standing up," she hissed.

"Yes, you are."

There was a little tug-of-war, and finally Blessing reclaimed her hand and crossed her arms, slouching back in her chair.

Damion frowned and then cleared his throat. "Well, with this being Christmas and all, and Christmas being a time for, you know, *family,* and all ..." He looked around from guest to guest, but his imploring eyes didn't land on one person for any length of time. "And with Christmas being about the *birth* of baby Jesus, and his mama being pregnant for the holidays and everything ..."

"What are you doing?" Blessing sizzled under her breath.

"Just hear me out, baby. Let me do this."

"We said we were gonna wait." She was talking through her teeth, but Kennedy could hear every word. Apparently, Carl and Sandy could, too. Carl was leaning back in his seat, his eyes wider than silver dollars. Sandy swayed slightly back and forth at the table, her face strained with a mixture of excitement and anxiety.

Damion cleared his throat again and wiped his hand on his forehead. "Wow. This is a lot harder than it looks. Ok, well, um, Carl ... Sandy ... Mr. and Mrs. Lindgren, I mean ..."

"Spit it out, man!" Carl finally blurted.

"Well, we're gonna have a baby."

Squeals of delight and a subdued applause sounded around the table. Sandy clasped her hands to her chest, but she glanced at Carl's serious face, and then she hid her smile behind her cider goblet. Damion and Blessing were arguing at each other in subdued tones, with Blessing's *I told you so* the only words Kennedy could make out.

Damion looked at Carl and wiped his forehead again, only this time with his napkin. "Um, so, Mr. Lindgren ... Carl ... I, uh, wanted to tell you that I know your daughter's really special to you, and she's really special to me, too, and I know that you being a pastor and all probably doesn't mean you want to have ... What I'm trying to say, sir, is I really want to do right by your daughter, by Blessing here."

"I know her name." Carl's tone was so flat you could have chopped veggies on it. Kennedy and Reuben raised their eyebrows at each other and stifled their giggles.

Damion dropped his napkin and glanced around the table imploringly. His gaze finally landed on Sandy. He gulped once before continuing. "And, so, to get to the point, sir ..."

"I wish you would."

Sandy hit Carl's uninjured arm with her napkin. "Hush, now, and let's hear what the poor boy has to say."

Kennedy could tell she was trying not to laugh, too.

Damion shifted his weight. "So, what I really want is I

want to ask Blessing to marry me."

Nobody spoke for several seconds. Kennedy was painfully aware of Reuben's presence next to her but didn't take her eyes off Blessing's boyfriend.

"I know it's maybe not the best time, but I thought, you know, Christmas being all about family and stuff ..."

"Yes." Carl spoke so quietly he had to repeat himself. "Yes."

Damion balked. "You mean ... you're saying it's ok?"

Carl took a sip of cider. "It's fine by me, man, but I'm not the one you need to ask."

Damion blinked at Carl a few times before his face lit up brighter than the lights on the Lindgrens' tree. He fumbled in his pockets and beamed down at Blessing. "Now you understand why I told you to get up?"

Still pouting but now blushing like a schoolgirl, Blessing stood and self-consciously tugged her miniskirt. Several women *awwed* when Damion dropped to his knee and opened the small black case he was holding. "Blessing Lindgren, will you marry me?"

She stole a quick glance at Sandy, who nodded encouragingly. Blessing wrapped one arm around her son and gave him a squeeze. "Well, squirt, what do you think? Should we say yes?"

Tyson jumped to his feet and wrapped both arms around Damion's neck. "Heck yeah!"

While Blessing chastised her son for his choice of words, Damion slipped the ring on her finger, and everyone clapped. A few started clinking their glasses demanding a kiss, and when Blessing and Damion complied, the table erupted in hoots and hollers, as well as quite a few snickers and one very loud *"Ew!"* from the kiddie table.

Kennedy shot a quick glance at Reuben, who was smiling along with everyone else. She couldn't remember a Christmas ever feeling quite so full, and it wasn't because of the piles of food she had heaped on her plate. After the holidays, she'd be right back where she started that week. There would be police reports. Long meetings with Drisklay and his cold cups of stale coffee. Interviews with men in drab suits and somber-toned ties from the district attorney's office.

But right now, none of that mattered. Right now, Kennedy was safe.

Right now, she was home.

ACKNOWLEDGEMENTS:

I'm thankful that while I was working on this story, the Lord provided many friends who graciously fielded all my random questions. Jonathan Patrick, a Las Vegas police officer, helped with a few of the cop scenarios to make sure I got the details as accurate as possible. Kaye Slater, a nursing lecturer at Gonzaga University, answered several medical questions about the injuries Kennedy and Carl experienced. William Troxel, a pastor as well as a volunteer EMT, helped me with the car crash scene and also helped me understand how the paramedics would respond. Louise Franklin was kind enough to share some of her own family history with me as I tried to create the backstories of Carl and Sandy. Annie Douglass Lima was a great help answering questions about Christmas in Kenya. She's also a fantastic editor.

I would also like to thank my friends — both real-life and virtual — who gave their great suggestions and critiques, and who more importantly prayed for me while I was working on Kennedy's story. My husband, as always, is my biggest support and encouragement, and I'm so thankful for the way he always urges me on, even when I'm feeling tired or sluggish.

Lastly, I'd like to publicly thank the Lord for sustaining me through yet another novel. I never imagined writing would be so physically, emotionally, and spiritually exhausting, but it is God who strengthens me and inspires me. I don't need a muse when I've got the Holy Spirit there, urging me on.

If you are a faithful reader and have followed my other books as well, I'd like to thank you for your support. And if this is your first time reading one of my novels, I'd like to thank you for giving me a try. If you want to know when I have a new release or would like to sign up for free books, please join the Alana Terry Readers' Club at alanaterry.com.

DISCUSSION QUESTIONS

Feel free to use these either in a book club or for personal journaling and reflection.

Story Questions – *Good for ice breakers.*

1. What is your most notable Christmas memory?

2. What is your worst holiday memory?

3. Think about how Kennedy and Reuben snuck behind the stage of the ballet. What is the most spontaneous (or mischievous) thing you have done with a friend?

4. Who is the craziest driver you know?

5. Have you ever been in a car accident? What happened?

6. Who was your most eccentric teacher or professor?

7. Are you a book lover like Kennedy? Pick a book you like. Tell why you like it and what that might tell others about your personality.

Issues Questions – *For those who want to go deeper.*

1. If you were Kennedy's pastor or parent and saw her struggles after her kidnapping, how would you counsel her?

2. Do you believe the church in general is a safe place for Christians to admit to mental health issues (depression, PTSD, anxiety, etc.)?

3. Why are some Christians, like Kennedy, reluctant to admit to issues like these?

4. How do you feel about Christians seeking medicine or secular therapy for a psychological issue like Post Traumatic Stress Disorder?

5. Do you agree with Kennedy's assumption that if she just prays more and reads her Bible more that God will heal her from her memories of the past?

6. If God could erase a painful memory from your life, would you ask him to do it?

7. Have you ever experienced God's healing, either physically or psychologically? Is there an area of your life in which you are still waiting for deeper healing?

8. Why do you think God allows some Christians to continue to struggle indefinitely with issues like depression or trauma, while others experience instantaneous healing or don't suffer from it at all?

Books by Alana Terry

North Korea Christian Suspense Novels

The Beloved Daughter

Slave Again

Torn Asunder

Flower Swallow

Kennedy Stern Christian Suspense Series

Unplanned

Paralyzed

Policed

Straightened

Turbulence

See a full list at www.alanaterry.com

Printed in the USA
CPSIA information can be obtained
at www.ICGtesting.com
JSHW030019100823
46269JS00002B/158